I0556299

LYCHOS

Book Three of The Lychos Cycle

PATTI LARSEN

Find out more about Patti Larsen at **pattilarsen.com**

ALSO BY

PATTI LARSEN

The Hayle Coven Universe

The Hunted Series
Fiona Fleming Cozy Mysteries
The Nightshade Cases
The Clone Chronicles
The Diamond City Trilogy
Didi and the Gunslinger

and much, much more.
Find your new favorite author at
pattilarsen.com
Sign up for new releases
bit.ly/pattilarsenemail

ONE

My legs ache, my whole body, really. I've been one tight, tense knot since leaving the train behind in the Northwest and stealing this family car. The long drive from southern Washington has given me nothing but time to think about what we've left behind—good friends, uncovered secrets and about what's to come. I crack open a window, allowing the cool Pennsylvanian night air, crisp with the promise of frost, to stir the heaviness inside. Heaviness matched by the weight in my heart, the burning need to reach this destination.

To reach Syd.

The small car smells of cat urine and spoiled milk. I ignore the stench, absorbed instead in the feeling of witch magic pulsing from the tree line before me. A secluded lane often visited by young lovers offers shelter as I block off my magic even further, just in case.

The big, black wolf shifts beside me, whining softly as his tongue makes a noisy journey across his chops. My fingers find the crescent shape of white fur on his shoulder and dig in. Sage loves it when I scratch the scar, moaning his lupine happiness at the attention though he is as intent as I am.

I haven't lost him. His mind remains intact, despite his transformation. We've come so far, he and I, the young, normal man I loved first bitten by a werewolf, made a revenant hated and feared by my people. I watched him, in our journey to find a cure to his condition, turn slowly from human to werewolf, without a trace of the tainted darkness that is the revenant's trademark. The very reason my people's werelaws demand his death.

Sage turns to meet my eyes, his still the beautiful sea green, though with the shape and depth of a wolf's. I can see the man he is inside him still, though I was certain his humanity would be gone forever. When he finally shifted into wereshape in the hills of southern California, just a few days ago, he felt perfect to me, more perfect than any werewolf I've ever met. The Hensley coven leader, Tallah, had surmised he is, rather than a soulless monster to be despised and dispatched, instead the next evolution of the werenation.

I can't help but agree with her. Though we have been

unable to reverse his transformation from full wolf back to human, the typical loss of self to animal, which usually happens to our kind, hasn't happened to my darling Sage. I feared that was the case, that I would lose him even when I fought so hard to keep him with me. Gave up everything I loved and the duty and honor my family demanded of me, to save him. It didn't seem fair we'd come so far only for Sage to devolve into the intelligence of a common wolf. Yes, they are brilliant, but they are animals.

My body reacts by scrunching low as I feel an Enforcer's power slip over our hiding place. The guardians of the North American Witch Council have been hunting us since we arrived on the continent. Like her European counterpart, Erica Plower has caved to the pressure of the werenation, agreeing to hunt us down and deliver Sage and me to the less-than-tender mercies of my fellow werewolves. So far, we've managed to elude them, thanks to dear friends and a lot of luck. I won't allow them to capture us now we're so close to ending this.

At least the Enforcers can't see us physically, nor magically, but the impulse to hide is too ingrained for me to stop. Sage pants softly next to me, almost cheerful in his demeanor, like this is fun for him.

He always had an odd sense of humor, and even more so now he's a wolf.

Wilding Springs lies beyond the trees. I originally

resisted coming here—a place that feels more like home than the palace in Ukraine—in the need to keep my dear friend, Sydlynn Hayle, and her coven out of my mess. She'd been trying ever since Sage and I escaped from the clutches of my people to track me down. But her touch went silent when Sage and I landed in North America, and I haven't heard from her since.

When I first thought Sage was a revenant, I did my best to keep my friends from becoming embroiled in this disaster, to protect them from my decision to try to save him. I have no idea what's become of Tallah and her family after the coven leader so openly protected us. Nor of my Steam Union friend, Piers Southway. The last I saw of him, he was unconscious, still in the wreck of the SUV he used to carry Sage and I to freedom. I can't think of them now, though the temptation to wallow in my worry is great.

The worst part is I now know Sage is no danger to anyone. That he is, in fact, much more than any other werewolf could hope to be. All of this hurt and heartache could have been avoided had I only known in the beginning. Now, I need help to convince the powers that be—the werenation, the witches—he is not a threat and to call off the hunt.

Sage needs to be safe so I can go home and save my grandfather from execution.

The wolf shifts beside me, leaning in to swipe the side

of my face with his tongue. He must feel my anxiety, smell it, because his mind reaches for mine, the barest touch so as not to trigger any power the patrolling Enforcers might pick up.

We can't sit here all night. Sage's voice is calm, composed, the practical tone of a wolf. My own chuffs her satisfaction at his words. *Any ideas?*

I've assessed and discarded at least a dozen since I pulled in and parked here only fifteen minutes ago. It's been a long journey from California to Pennsylvania and I'm glad to be almost done with it. I need rest—we both do—and anger grinds my teeth together, frustration that the witches in black robes watching over Wilding Springs are keeping me from my destination.

We could just call her out here, Sage sends. *Syd would come in a heartbeat.*

Alerting the Enforcers we're here, I send, scratching his mane with absent fingers. My lower lip hurts from chewing on it, eyes narrowed as I grip the steering wheel with my free hand so tightly my palm cramps. Every scenario I've come up with puts the coven in harm's way. If I can only get to Syd and tell her what's happened, find some neutral ground to talk to Femke Svennson, the leader of the European Council. I might be able to diffuse this enough to get Sage a pass so we can travel back to Ukraine and make sure my grandfather is safe.

I've been warned to stay away until the time is right,

whatever that means. The odd young woman I met in California, Zoe Helios, claims to be an Oracle, to see the future. She warned me against returning too soon, that doing so would mean the permanent enslavement of my people. But according to Piers, Oleksander is under arrest, his execution imminent, all thanks to his support of me after I became a fugitive.

For all I know, Oleksander is already dead. But I refuse to believe it. Regardless of my grandfather's state, I will go home and ensure the throne of the werenation never serves as a seat for the revenant pretender, Cicero Caine. I shudder at the thought of the huge Californian pack leader taking his place where my grandfather should rightfully sit. I can only hope the werenation rejects him as a candidate, and that the gathering of the packs takes far longer than I need to sort out this mess with Sage.

We could just go to the council leader here, Sage sends. *We both know I'm not a danger to anyone.*

I shake my head. *Not an option*, I send. Erica Plower might be a Hayle witch, but I've never trusted her. Syd's the only one strong enough to keep the peace for any length of time. And she can be very persuasive. Not to mention she's saved the Universe who knew how many times. The magic races owe her.

I owe her.

Another pass of power makes me snarl. Syd can't be home. If she was, she'd be out here, giving these

Enforcers grief. I've seen her do it in the past, back when her mother, Miriam, was Council Leader and under the control of the Brotherhood.

Thinking of them makes me even angrier and I need to focus. But it's difficult, knowing they are behind this wretched mess, if only by association. Though I have no proof of our guesses and suppositions, the general consensus among my friends is that Caine and his pack are the creation of Liander Belaisle, the leader of the fallen Brotherhood of sorcerers and that his protégé, Rupe, has been trying to recreate what his master made.

New werewolves, the first in centuries. Not since the Black Souls made us have weres been created. Only those born to our lineage are permitted to live. Our bite is viral, infectious, but only to humans, normals. Which leads us full circle to Sage and the reason we're on the run.

I glance sideways at him, hating that my mind always takes this turnabout. The endless cyclical stirring of thought leads me from my grandfather to Caine to the Brotherhood and, finally, to Sage and his safety. I'm meant to be werequeen one day, but I can barely keep one wolf safe.

I figure we have a few options, Sage sends. *We can turn ourselves in.*

After all we've been through? We both snort together. Not going to happen.

We can call for Syd. Again, not a choice I'm willing to

risk, unless it's absolutely last resort.

We can try to sneak in, Sage sends.

Past all that magic. I sigh and rub my arms with both hands, the thin jacket I stole from the back seat of our liberated car barely enough to keep the September evening chill from my skin. *We might as well just give in*, I send. *They'll be on us the moment we try to cross.*

Even if you take us through the veil? Sage's eyes are so wise, I become lost in them a moment before shaking my head.

Can't, I send, bitterly disappointed by the fact. *We've tried all along, remember? For whatever reason, I can cut into it, but not through it.*

Sage's muzzle dips, forehead pushing against my shoulder. *I think I figured out why.* His nose is cold and wet, but I don't flinch from the touch on my hand. *Remember when you took us to California? When we were being attacked by the hunters?*

I do. It was our only successful jump. Without help, that is. Our first dive into the veil left us stranded in the dark, rubbery membrane between planes. Thankfully, a drach had been close by and rescued us. Otherwise, I'm certain we would have been lost there forever.

You used me to complete the trip, he sends. My head snaps up as he goes on. *I could feel the drain on my energy, felt you with me. I'm right, aren't I?*

My mouth hangs open a moment before I grasp his

furry face in my hands and kiss his snout. *Brilliant*, I send. *Why didn't I think of that?*

I can only guess it's because we're both stressed and tired, Sage sends, practicality tinted with humor. *Can't blame us for forgetting.*

Me, he means. He's so kind, even now.

My wolf reaches for his and finds only Sage. Of course. He's fully integrated, unlike me. When Syd freed my people from the controls of the Black Soul sorcerers who created us, she also freed our magic. But I've always felt a disconnect, as though there are parts of my power I can't yet access. Sage doesn't have that flaw.

More to consider when this is all over and I have time to think.

Can we do it? Sage's magic is ready and willing, a deep and powerful river of deliciousness I wish I could dive into and never emerge from.

I think so. My wolf barks an affirmative. With the boost of his magic, with both of us tied to the demon power Syd claims allows us access to the veil, I'm sure we can make it through.

That still doesn't solve our problem. *They'll feel us use our magic*, I send.

Sage bobs his head. *That's the only downfall*, he sends. *So any way we look at it, we're going to get caught.* He sighs, the hot puff of his breath on my cheek as he licks me. *If only there were some way to hide the power we use.*

The image of a dark and quiet cavern enters my mind, a gasp of air pulling me around to hug Sage close to me. His wolf body quivers as he catches my excitement and when I pull back to grin at him, his tongue lolls out of the side of his mouth in a wolf grin.

You, I send, *are a genius.*

TWO

I slip from the driver's seat and into the darkness, Sage padding out beside me on silent wolf feet. It's late, well after 1AM, all the amorous lovers who might use this lookout long gone home. The trees part in the distance, a cliff giving an excellent view of the town below. I catch a whiff of Enforcer magic as Sage tucks close to me, huge head tall enough to reach my waist.

We move as one, quiet and stealthy, abandoning our ride for the edge of the trees. I know enough to stay hidden from prying Enforcer eyes as well as their magic, though we will have to time things perfectly if we expect to keep our arrival a secret for any length of time.

It feels odd to travel with Sage this way and yet not. How strange I feel more comfortable with him in this shape than I ever have with his human form. He's very calm and seems to love being a wolf. At least, he tells me so every time I ask him in a moment of weakness and guilt.

It took me two days to accept he wasn't losing his humanity, and another full one to embrace the fact he is more himself now than he has ever been. I have never believed in fate or destiny outside of the duty I must fulfill, but with Sage, I feel now he was born to be a wolf. I can only hope his poise and power can convince the councils and my people Sage is worthy of life. More, that he is a new creature who deserves to be respected and embraced.

This could all be over in a matter of minutes. I feel my heart begin to race as I look ahead, to success, before reining myself in. We are far from done, and though this plan might work, there is a very good chance it will also land us in the custody of the waiting Enforcers. Will they ask questions before attacking? It will depend on their orders. I didn't exactly give Pender reason to trust me the last time we met. Enforcer Leader Tremere isn't a terrible man, or a cruel one. But he follows orders. If Erica has decided we are too much of a problem to deal with, she might act impulsively.

Though I would feel very sorry for her, indeed, should anything bad happen to Sage or me on her watch. I am my own woman and far from a coward, but even I am afraid of Syd when she's angry.

It's hard not to let myself dream this might work, though, especially when we come to a halt inside the thin tree line and I look down over Wilding Springs. My gaze picks out Town Hall and the library inside, my heart constricting for the loss of Liam O'Dane and the birth of Syd's son, Gabriel. I lift my head to glare at the Hilltop Hotel, the place of my first meeting with Syd and her family, the moment I realized there were witches who could be trusted and the freedom I longed for might not be just a far-off dream.

But when I look down again, I focus on one thing only. Not the white two-story with the big back yard bordering the small park. I'll be there before long. No, instead I look south and west, to the edge of town and the darkness hiding the cavern where once a monster died.

Cesard, the Firbolg magician and his supernatural hitchhikers are long gone, though the vampire essence that possessed him now lives in Syd. But the cavern which served as his prison remains, the ancient wards blocking elemental magic still firmly in place. Syd has sheltered it with energy, kept it hidden all these years, but only to those who aren't aware of its existence.

It's the perfect answer, if this works. Walking in is no good. The barrier of power the Enforcers have around Wilding Springs will alert them if anyone passes, and they'll be on us before we can escape. But this way, if I can ride us through the veil to its depths, there is a chance the power I use will be swallowed by the suppressing wards of the cavern. There are no guarantees, but I don't expect any. At the very least, if the Enforcers do feel me open the veil, they won't know where I've gone and no amount of searching will discover us. That way, I don't put the Hayle coven at risk. Yes, Syd's magic and the power of the family might disguise our arrival behind the wards surrounding Syd's house, but there's no promise the Enforcers won't feel Sage and me anyway. The cavern blocks all power, giving us at least a ray of hope to grasp. If we can make it there, smother our path, we can then simply make our way on foot to Syd.

Hopefully, if they feel our passing, the Enforcers will think it's only Syd returning, though Pender is now aware I have access to the veil.

So many ifs and maybes, and yet this is our only viable option. I will not get caught, not now. Not when the end is so close at hand. I can almost taste Caine's blood in my mouth, teeth clamping together at the thought of ripping out his throat. Of rescuing my grandfather and making sure he is firmly on his throne. And, if I'm forgiven, bowing to his need and retaking my place as wereprincess.

I can't think of what will happen to Sage, even if he is allowed to live. But in my best case scenario, he will at least be alive.

Sage butts my hand with his head. *I know you want to go home*, he sends. He's been in my mind, the devil, though I'm fine with it, oddly. *But you can't yet*. His green eyes are dark in the moonless night.

A stab of pain hits me as I again think of the dark-haired girl from California. I've tried to wall off the words of the young oracle girl. Zoe Helios's prediction the werenation will fall if I return too soon burns holes in my optimism. He had to remind me when I'm ready to believe in success, didn't he? But Sage is as practical as a wolf and stands there, supporting me, as I shiver and cling to his fur, my grandfather's beloved face in my mind. *Really, Charlie*, he sends ever so softly. *You have to stop doing this to yourself. It's not your fault.*

I nod, saliva filling my mouth as my stomach rebels. *I know*, I send, though my heart screams it is, it *is* all my fault. I brought this on all of us, by my selfishness, by refusing to let go of Sage when I should have. I could have dealt with Caine and his people. Even that bastard, Andre Dumont, and his despicable sons, without the worry and stress of trying to keep Sage safe. If only I hadn't been so weak.

Sage stares at me in silence, tail curled around him where he sits in the scrub, black fur blending him into the night. When I'm finally dovetailing down into self-hate and being devoured by my guilt, he leans close and nips my leg. I cry out at the pain, not so much because it hurt, but because the sensation pulls me out of my inner torture.

Enough, he sends. *We have a job to do.*

A job that doesn't involve going back to Ukraine to rescue my grandfather. How am I supposed to know when the time is right to return? Zoe never told me that. Am I supposed to guess? She mentioned a great trauma I must endure, but I will survive. Could it be my grandfather's death she means? Must I wait until Oleksander is killed before returning? If so, it will be to avenge his murder and take Caine down. If it's the last thing I do on this earth.

All of that is for later. I will put Sage first one last time, get him to safety, his situation sorted. And then I will deal with the revenants, the sorcerer-made pack who has invaded my werenation. And make sure they don't survive the attention.

I reach for the veil, feel the fire in me burn, sizzle. It's hotter now, since I spoke with Zoe. She, too, uses flame, though hers seemed to want to consume her, to devour me along with her. I can still feel her touch as I tap into the elemental power of my demon influence even as I tense and wait.

We stand in utter silence, Sage's head tilted to the side, ears perked, a wolf statue with a white crescent scar on his shoulder. The wait seems to take forever before magic pulses over us, the Enforcer's pass of power ebbing and flowing around me. They have no idea we are here. The feeling of the magic is calm, almost bored, routine. I hope such blasé focus will serve to our advantage.

One breath after the magic has passed over us I grasp Sage's magic in mine. He softly bonds us together, rendering my grip on him unnecessary. I almost laugh, slightly giddy at the connection. He's so beautiful inside.

It's Sage who reaches for the veil, a subtle touch. I take over, slicing it cleanly first on our end, then the other, knowing exactly where I'm going. The boost of his power is more than enough. We leap through together though, just as I pass through, I'm certain I feel the pressure of Enforcer magic snapping to attention. The veil slurps shut before I can know for sure even as I drop to my knees in the dark beside the shaggy form of the black wolf.

THREE

I feel dull and empty, suddenly, the ache of where my magic usually resides dead in my chest. Sage shakes his head, paws the ground, then his ear as though in distress. I comfort him with a quick hug, gasping my own loss.

"It's all right," I say out loud in the echoing quiet of the cavern, the dirt and stone floor cold under my knees, even through my jeans. I reach for his mind and come up blank. Sage licks his chops nervously, tail hitting me hard as he swings around then back to me. "I know, that's the point. This place suppresses magic." I look up at the perma-glow of the suspended witchlight overhead, smell the old taint of the demon who was trapped here, the magician and the vampire. "We need to stay a bit. I think they felt us cross."

Sage pants heavily, but nods even as relief rushes

through me. I can't hear him and the cavern suppresses power. There is a chance this place could have turned him into a simple wolf after all, something at which even his transformation hadn't succeeded. I know it was a slim chance, but seeing him respond to me assures me he's still in there. Sage is still with me, though I can't hear him in my head or feel his power.

He crouches next to me, shivering, whining softly on occasion as I hug him close and bury my face in his fur. I might not be able to feel his magic, but his solid wolf form is comforting nonetheless.

I could have made a terrible mistake bringing us here. If the Enforcers tracked us after all, they could be on us at any second. And they would have us trapped, powerless. Surely, they know about this cavern? But as the seconds tick by and only the quiet of the cave embraces us, I finally relax and ease back from Sage.

"They might know someone crossed the veil," I say, "but they either don't have the nerve to come into Syd's territory to check, or they assume it's her." Hopefully, the second. They have to be tracking her movements, though. So if she's not here, if she's off on another plane or in the veil helping the drach leader, Max, the Enforcers will know something is up.

No more time to wait. I have to risk it.

I stand, ruffling Sage's fur. "You'll be safe here," I say. "I'm going to run to the house and talk to Syd. As long as you remain inside the cavern, they won't be able to find you." If they capture me, I will never reveal his location.

Sage shakes his big head, growling at me, showing his teeth. He stands and paces toward the exit, a dark tunnel leading off toward the surface. It's difficult not to roll my eyes, but I do toss my hands and shrug. We've been in this together from the first. I guess I can see his point.

Sage pauses at the tunnel mouth, looking back at me and I nod and follow him.

A huge breath escapes me as I lean against the boulder guarding the exit and shove it aside. It rolls easily, releasing Sage and I into the outdoors, our magic back—to my gasping relief—into full power.

It's warmer outside than I remember, the valley where Wilding Springs was built holding in more of the autumn heat than the ridge where we parked our stolen car. I return the guardian rock to its place and ease through the trees on the way toward the center of town. We can't risk another veil ride, not inside the bounds of Syd's territory. We'd draw Enforcers, for certain. I feel around ahead of me, grateful to have my magic back and to have Sage's power linked once more to mine.

Sage moves with the confidence of experience and I remember then, with a little shake of my head, I'm not the only one who has lived here. He's spent the last several years running the dojo downtown, his small apartment over the studio our secret rendezvous. I don't have to guide him. He knows this place as well as I do.

How easily I forget this isn't just about me. Yes, I put Sage first when I chose to save him, but I fall so easily into the singular protection mode I was taught from childhood. Without a bonded master to protect, I'm supposed to be number one, my needs and my goals those of the pack and the throne. But Sage is his own person—wolf—and I have to keep reminding myself he has his own path to walk.

The park is dark, the small copse of trees near the back end the perfect entry point. I circle the subdivision where Syd's house stands, choosing to enter through the yard instead of taking the street. While the feeling of Enforcers remains outside the familiar touch of Syd's magic, I refuse to take chances.

The closer we get to the coven's main house, the stronger the Hayle power becomes and I feel it welcome me. I shush it softly with a touch of energy, hating the risk, but knowing without it all kinds of alarms could be raised. Better to let the family magic accept my presence than set off the wards protecting the family.

Sage hugs the line of trees bordering the park, staying at my side while I slip through the shadows, eyes everywhere as I wait for an attack that never comes. By the time we slide past the family wards and into the back yard at Syd's house, I'm wound tight and ready to fly.

The shielding embraces me, hugs me with love. Syd's made sure the family magic knows me as well as any coven member, and I'm grateful now for her thoughtfulness. I reach through it, feeling for her, knowing before I do she's not here. If she were, she'd be in the yard by now, alerted by the family power I arrived. Instead, I quiver like a hunted animal, clinging to the comfort of the coven's magic even as I contemplate running.

This was a bad idea. She's not here. And I won't put the rest of the family at risk without her around to protect them.

Sage seems to agree, backing up a few steps. We'll have to retreat to the cavern and come up with a new plan. Or wait for Syd to come back.

The back door opens, the motion-sensitive light coming on. I duck quickly to the side, hiding in the shadows with Sage shaking beside me, while a dark figure steps out into the yard. She looks worried, one hand clutching the door, the other clenched at her side. Dark, straight hair shivers around her as she takes another half-step onto the patio stones, the light reflecting from her dusky skin.

"Charlotte?" Sashenka Hensley's whisper carries into the night, backed by a thread of power, seeking me. I block off from habit as Syd's second—Tallah's sister—raises her free hand to clutch at the throat of her robe.

She's dressed for bed, feet bare, but she looks wide awake. "Charlotte, is that you?"

I hesitate, not because I don't trust Shenka. I do. Syd chose her for a reason, to care for the coven when she's not here. But I need Syd, damn it. Where is she?

"It's okay," she continues, still whispering. "I know you're afraid. But I also know you'd want to hear this." She pauses, looks around, steps out further, letting the door close behind her. "Piers is okay."

I choke on a silent sob, crumpling to hug Sage who licks my cheek. I've been so worried about the blond sorcerer, the relief of knowing he's not harmed is almost worse than a blow.

"He told us you were probably coming this way." Shenka releases the chokehold she has on her robe and holds out both hands. "Syd's not here, but you are always welcome. Let us protect you."

I shake my head in the dark. I can't do this, can't risk it. Not with the kids in the house. What if the Enforcers come? I won't put Gabriel or Syd's daughter, Ethie, in harm's way.

"Please," Shenka whispers. "Trust us. Syd would want it this way." One last pause. "You're family, Charlotte."

She had to say that, didn't she? I feel myself caving even as my traitor feet carry me out of the dark and into the light. Shenka doesn't move, still holding out her hands. The last three steps I run, hugging her tight as she clutches me close, her face wet with tears as she kisses my cheek.

"Oh, Charlotte," she says. "Welcome home."

FOUR

The back door swings shut behind me as I enter the familiar house, pacing down the hall toward the stairs. Quaid is just descending, catches me as he hits the bottom, pulling me into a giant hug that lifts me from my feet. I kiss him soundly on the lips, knowing Syd won't mind, wiping tears of my own from my face with impatient hands. Quaid hugs me again, one big hand on my back, the other tangled in the cropped off mess I made of my hair.

"You're okay." He's choked up, deep voice rough. "We were worried."

I nod into his broad chest, the scent of chocolate and spices warming me. "Me, too."

Something hits my leg and I pull back from Syd's husband to discover a very angry silver Persian perched on my foot. His round body quivers, fur on end, ears flat back as fire flares in his amber eyes.

"Charlotte," he snarls. "You are in so much trouble, young lady, I can't even tell you."

I bend and scoop him up, hugging him though he hisses and spits at me, batting my face with his silver paws—claws retracted, so I know he's not really angry—and kiss his furry forehead.

"Sass," I whisper into his fur.

The Hayle family magic tightens around me even as Sassafras's demon power triggers my own fire element.

"Don't ever do anything that stupid ever again," he says. "I mean it."

I turn him to face Sage. "No promises."

Sass sighs and relaxes in my arms at last. "I suppose this is the boy in question?" That almost makes me laugh. The demon cat has such a way with words.

"This is Sage," I say as the big wolf dips his head. "Sage, you know Shenka, I think?" Surely he's met her once or twice? Syd's been training with him for years now, I can't imagine she didn't take her second to the dojo a time or two. "Quaid?"

The big witch shrugs. "We met," he says, dark eyes fixed on Sage. "Welcome."

26

"The kids." I turn on Quaid who shakes his head, finger on his lips.

"Galleytrot is with them," he says, voice low. Gabriel and Ethie must be asleep, the big hound of the Wild Hunt their constant guardian. "Let's go downstairs."

The basement. Of course, it will be safer there, hidden in the layers of protections around the family's main pentagram. I follow Shenka, still carrying the Persian, hearing the soft pad of Sage's paws behind me as I pass through the kitchen and down into the cellar.

The cold concrete floor is etched and painted with a giant white pentagram, the single bulb illuminating the large space casting wide shadows into the corners. I finally set Sass down in the middle of the room and turn to face Shenka and Quaid, one hand falling to Sage's broad head.

Thank you for taking us in. Sage's mental voice is strong and I know from the nod Quaid gives him, from the way Sass fluffs his fur, they've all heard his words. *We know this is putting you in danger and that's the last thing we want.* He looks up at me. *But things have developed we need to share, things that will hopefully change our situation for the better.*

Sassafras swipes one paw over his whiskers before wrapping his fluffy tail around his paws, amber eyes flaring with magic. "I assume," he says in his most droll demon boy voice, "you're referring to the fact you have, as of yet, to devolve into a soulless monster bent on killing everyone in sight?"

Sage bows his head to the cat with a wolfish smile. *Clever*, he says.

"For a human boy," Sass says, "you're not so bad yourself." He cocks his head to one side. "And rather accepting of a talking cat, at that."

Sage coughs a laugh, his paw rising to his nose. *I'd be a bit of a hypocrite if I didn't accept such things are possible.*

"Touché," Sass says before winking one eye at me. "You can keep this one."

If only it is that easy. But Sass's approval means a lot to me, as does Shenka's smile and Quaid's grim grin.

"We used the veil to get here," I say, "but the Enforcers might still know we've crossed." I fill them in on our little plan to use the cavern and Quaid nods.

"Brilliant, actually," he says. "They might come looking, but they'll have no proof you arrived here. We'll keep it that way." He's a former Enforcer trainee, thinks like them still. He hasn't completely relaxed, but at least he's not freaking out, so we probably have some time.

"The family magic understands how important it is to keep you two safe," Shenka says, blue fire forming at her feet before fading away.

I nod to her, gratitude surfacing so powerfully I'm unable to speak. I do release a soft squeak as a black tunnel forms beside Quaid and though my heart soars at the thought it might be a familiar face, the two who emerge don't fit my expectations. I realize then how much I miss Piers as Ethpeal and Demetrius step clear of the sorcery pathway and join us.

She comes to me, hugs me firmly, though without judgment or any emotion beyond grim joy. I kiss her cheek, Syd's grandmother's blue eyes meeting mine as she pulls away. There are delicate threads of silver in her black hair, but she is as stunning as she has been since her transformation by her own sorcery.

"Hello, girl," she says.

"Hello, Ethpeal." I gesture at the big lupine beside me. "This is Sage."

She bows her head to him. "Well now," she says. "I suppose he'll do."

More endorsements. I love this family.

Ethpeal turns, including the others in our conversation as Demetrius slips forward quickly and quietly to kiss my cheek, his cherub face smiling, pale blue eyes shining with happiness. I squeeze his strong hand as his wife speaks.

"We just missed you out there," she says to me, gesturing vaguely beyond the basement walls. "We almost grabbed the pair of you ourselves, but you beat us to it." She pokes the end of my nose with one finger. "Clever girl," she says. "The cavern was an excellent choice. But the Enforcers know something is up." She shakes her head. "I did my best to muddy your passing, but I have a feeling they'll be by before too long."

We have to go. I flinch, almost take a step to leave, but Demetrius is still holding my hand and he won't release me. And Ethpeal steps in to block me as I try to move forward, intense gaze narrowed. I know better than to argue with her.

I won't win.

"Where is Syd?" Maybe I shouldn't cling to the need I feel to see her, to explain all of this to her. These very capable witches and sorcerers are here now, for me, willing to help. But my irrational side wants Syd to protect them since I can't.

Quaid shows his first signs of anxiety, hands deep in his front pockets, shoulders hunching forward so his dark t-shirt bunches over his broad chest. "We don't know," he says in his deep and steady voice, it at least not betraying his nervousness. "She left with Max three days ago and hasn't come home." Chocolate brown eyes meet mine. "They are still fighting infestations of creatures from the Dark Universe, ones that crossed when Demonicon fell." I slip my hand through Sage's fur, the other tightening on Demetrius. Syd's little sister is the Ruler of Demonicon and went through her own trial by fire, losing her world to a cult only to pull it back together again. She's a true Hayle, like her sister, though the damage done did a number on the veil between worlds. Since Syd's son, Gabriel, opened a gateway to the other

Universe, the drach have been doing their best to repair the damage. The assault on Demonicon didn't help matters. And though things are mostly back to normal, I know there is still much to be done to restore order and finish healing the hurts done to the veil.

I wanted to tell this story to Syd. But the family gathered is watching me, waiting for me to fill them in on everything that's happened. I'm a little surprised Tallah hasn't been in touch with her sister and I can see from the worry on her face, she is, too. If they are willing to risk their lives for Sage and me, the least I can do is tell them everything.

FIVE

Sage begins before I get the chance, showing and explaining what happened to him in Europe. I wince when he shares the experience of being bitten. It's the first time he's allowed me to know what really occurred. I'm with him on the dark road heading for the hostel, feel his sadness as he thinks of me, the way his heart rate leaps as a dark shape throws itself from the forest and lands on him—

"A wolf!" I gasp the word, looking down at him. "You said it at the time, but no one believed you." But it's true. The form that bit him was lupine, not a wereshape.

Sage nods. *Does that mean something?*

I don't know. "I've always been told turning full wolf

means the end of my humanity." The wolf in Sage's image is huge, dark with red tones and has the feel of Caine. But that means he's able to shift from human form to full wolf without losing himself. How is that possible?

Demetrius shrugs, blue eyes thoughtful. "There is so much we don't know about your people," he says. "Now your race is free of the Black Souls, is it possible to shift fully without harm?"

I shudder from the idea, but it's not without merit when I force myself to consider it. I look at Sage, churning questions turning into growing revelation. Could the bite he sustained have been different because of the form Caine took?

Answers later. I must inform the others of what we've endured first if I'm to have their aid figuring this out.

The moment I begin, they all listen quietly as I tell them everything. I've been known to hold back details, to protect myself from full disclosure and what that might mean. No one needs to know all the hurt I've felt. But as I stand there with Demetrius's hand in mine and Ethpeal watching me with her steady gaze, I find myself telling them intimate details about the Dumonts and their ownership of me, about my grandfather and my father's desertion leaving me stuck as heir to the throne, and my fears for Sage. My hatred for Caine. And all the supposition Tallah and I worked out in her sunny kitchen in California.

Ethpeal's eyes tighten at the mention of Belaisle. "Impossible," she says. "And yet."

Demetrius nods, gaze bright but not with good emotions. "There's still a chance he's out there," he says. He almost sounds happy. Considering Belaisle tortured and turned Demetrius, forced him to serve, to betray those he cared about, I can understand completely his desire for Belaisle to be alive. So he can kill him personally.

We're very much alike, Demetrius and I. He has a wolf in him, somewhere, I'm certain.

"Tallah's guesswork is sound," Ethpeal says, now pacing in a small circuit that reminds me of Syd so much I relax slightly. This was the right choice after all. "It would be just like Belaisle to want his own army. It's quite possible he set the werewolf program in motion long before his battle with Syd." She nods to herself, fingers plucking at her lower lip. "And there is nothing to say Rupe would have to remain loyal. If something happened to Liander, Rupe is arrogant enough to think he could fill his master's shoes."

"That doesn't answer why Sage is different." Quaid's shoulders go back, head tilting as he observes the quiet wolf. "What happened to make this work?"

"That's what Rupe wants to know," I say. "Why we think he tried to kidnap Sage."

"You said the revenants in Europe felt different."

Shenka's frown looks like her sister's and I realize they are far more alike than either would willingly admit. "They weren't crazy, either."

I shake my head. "The one I met felt like he was in pain, more than insane. But nothing like Sage."

"Logical," she says. "Considering Syd freed you from sorcery."

"How's that?" Ethpeal spins on her, suddenly intent.

Shenka seems nervous, though she smiles through it as she always does. "I only meant," she said, "now that the werewolves aren't contained and controlled by sorcery, everything about them is different. So the infection they pass on would be changed too, wouldn't it?"

I nod. I've thought of this, though I didn't explore the idea very far. But she's right. It's not just our way of being that's different. It's everything about us.

"Go on." Ethpeal waves at her. "Work the idea through."

Shenka dimples before returning to her thoughtful frown. "I'm wondering," she says, "if the Black Souls did this to you on purpose."

Did what? Sage shifts where he stands, his black furred tail touching Sass's white. The cat doesn't flinch, amber eyes focused on Syd's second.

"The infection." She looks around at all of us. "They wanted to control you, how you reproduce. So they made it impossible for you to make other werewolves outside of natural birth."

Quaid shakes his head. "Then why make their bite infectious at all?"

Shenka clearly doesn't have an answer and I feel a little silly for focusing on her so intently. Until Demetrius snaps his fingers with an impish grin.

"They screwed up," he says, letting go of my hand at last. I miss the warmth of his skin as he rubs his together. "They tried to control too many variables, didn't they?" His chuckle makes me smile, though I have no idea what he's talking about. He turns on Sage. "I bet," he says, eyes twinkling, "you don't carry that infection, my boy."

Why wouldn't I? Sage's ears perk. *I'm a werewolf.*

"You're something else entirely," Demetrius says. "I've been investigating the both of you," he winks, "with apologies." I feel his sorcery retreat, though completely missed the intrusion. I forget just how skilled the small sorcerer is, still at times thinking of him as the mad, damaged man on whom Syd took pity. But he is that deranged creature no longer, and from the twinkle in his eyes, he's pleased with himself. "I just had to see what makes you tick. And I have to say, I'm intrigued by your design."

I should be insulted, I suppose, he's taken such a liberty. But I'm more interested in the excitement in his voice. "What do you mean?"

He opens his hands, a small, black wolf made of wisps of darkness appearing. "From what I can sense— and what I know of the Black Souls—your species were constructed from a variety of powers," he says. "Demon for strength and the fire of anger, witch for access to the elements on the most basic level. And sorcery." The little figure transforms into a werewolf, a man, and back again. "The sorcery was yours, as it is for all creatures, we've been told." The first magic, if the drach were to be believed, inherent in all living things. "But the Black Souls knew if they were to control you, they needed to corrupt your natural power. The addition of demon and witch magic they twisted for their use. They wanted to create you and let you breed. They didn't expect the byproduct of the danger of your bite."

"The infection," I say.

He nods. "It's not a real illness," he says. "It's a passing on of power. But if it's passed on to one who doesn't have their sorcery activated, it corrupts and destroys instead of building, triggering that innate power to devour everything, including the soul of the infected."

Ethpeal is frowning. "I think I see where you're going," she says.

Demetrius beams at her. "And when they discovered the flaw, it was too late. From what I can feel of you two," he points at us, "no matter your origins, the power they gave you, woke in you through birth or bite, is unalterable." I feel his sorcery push against my wolf and she growls and pushes back. "Their own invention with the built-in ability to turn against them. Once they made werewolves, they couldn't change you."

"They could have just destroyed us." I'm surprised they didn't.

"Who knows why the Black Souls did what they did," Demetrius says, no longer smiling. I can tell from his stance, the way his hands quiver at his sides, he had dealings with the Czar and his people before Belaisle destroyed his mind, and possibly after. "They may have been thrilled with the discovery the bite of their creations destroyed human souls. How delightful. And as long as they kept you afraid of your infection and in control, they had nothing to worry about." His tone is dark and sad.

"But now that Syd has freed us?" I'm almost afraid to ask. How much more is there to uncover about my people? And are we too hidebound to accept the way things are? Our laws and the way we cling to them tell me these revelations could cause serious division in the packs.

"I don't know." Demetrius shrugs, smiling, happy again. "But I can tell you, I'm right. Sage isn't infectious."

Sage isn't… I grin at his words. "He's not?"

He flicks his fingers at imaginary dust on his sleeve. "Told you, didn't I? And you had doubts."

I lunge for him and kissed his cheek. He blushes and

touches his face, blue eyes sparkling.

"You're sure?" How can this be possible? Is Sage really that different from me?

"I'm sure." He glances at Ethpeal. "Now we need to find out why and how to pass it on."

No longer infectious. Imagine if my people were free of the fear of infecting normals. "That means revenants would be a thing of the past." My people would no longer have to fear, though new laws will have to be made. Laws like those that govern the creation of new vampires. But those laws can come later, when level heads are able to think things through.

As long as it's our level heads that are doing the thinking.

"The kind you're referring to already are." Demetrius frowns. "The soulless kind. The sorcery the Black Souls used to make you no longer seems to eat everything in its path, absorbed by the buried power in normals. If your encounters with the revenant you met in Europe is any indication. But the Brotherhood—or Rupe—are still trying to make werewolves. And likely making the same mistakes the Black Souls did without knowing how to control the sorcery in the normals they are using as guinea pigs."

"When we were under the Black Soul's control," I say, working it through in my head, "the bite of a werewolf, in wereform, turned normals into revenants because their magic was woken the wrong way."

"Correct," Demetrius says. "The sorcery of the werebite triggered the wakening of the normal's sorcery, but created a cascade effect, a devouring, rather than a true wakening. Thus the soullessness and insanity."

And the difference. "So they don't go crazy," I say.

"No," Demetrius says. "They just don't survive."

"But now we're free," I say, feeling my stomach loosen its tension as understanding unravels, "the bite of a werewolf does... what?"

"Creates a werewolf," Demetrius says, "but one unable to form fully, from your descriptions. They no longer have the emptiness of true revenants, but there is still a flaw in their design."

"So the fact I was bitten by a full wolf," Sage says, "made all the difference?"

"I believe so," the sorcerer says, repeating what I've already begun to consider. "The infection of the wereform seems to have altered itself when in full wolf form. To something that can be transmitted without ill effect."

This is ground shaking, massive. Oleksander needs to know.

Oleksander.

"I have to go home." Desperation bursts to life inside me. "I have to save my grandfather." I finish my story, tell them of Zoe and her warning. Ethpeal and Demetrius are both intent on me as Shenka covers her mouth with one hand, distress in her dark eyes and Quaid turns sideways from me, head down.

"I've heard of the Oracles," Demetrius says, frowning for the first time. "But I thought them extinct long ago. This is troubling, Charlotte. But I can tell you now, if she warned you, you must heed her. And stay away."

I shake my head in denial, begging him with my eyes to change his opinion. Why I care what a tiny, cherub-faced man with curly white hair and kind blue eyes says is beyond me. Except I know he's been through more than any of us and would never lie to me or lead me false.

We will go back to Ukraine, Sage sends in a firm tone. *Once this is sorted out. And we'll free Oleksander and kick Caine's ass all the way to hell.*

I look down at him, shaking, knowing he's right and that I must listen.

There's only one way to do that, he goes on. *I must prove myself to the Councils. That I'm not a threat. And prove Caine is.*

"You have a plan, I take it, wolf boy?" Sassafras's sarcasm actually makes me feel better, as does the use of the nickname Piers coined for Sage.

Sage bares his teeth in a grin. *I do, cat*, he sends. *I have to show them I'm okay. Let them examine me. But it will go much better if there are two of us.*

I stare at him in confusion. "We're not infecting someone else," I say.

41

Sage shakes his big head, the scent of his fur carrying to me, calming. *No, silly*, he says. *I'm talking about you, Charlotte. You have to finish your transformation to full wolf and show them everything is changed.*

SIX

Sage has lost his mind, after all.

"I can't." I take a step back from him, chest tight with fear. If I let myself become a full wolf, I'll be lost, an animal. He's not gone, I know that, but I'm different from him. I was born a werewolf, not created by this new means Belaisle and Rupe have concocted. I'll be gone, my humanity given to the wolf and I will never, ever, return.

Won't I?

Charlie, Sage sends, standing, shaking himself before fixing his green eyes on me. *Says who?*

Says... centuries of werelore. Says the Black Souls.

I cough, choke, try to breathe as anger and deep, echoing sadness bubble around inside me, aimed at the horrible sorcerers who enslaved my people, not just with their magic, but with the power of belief. Even now,

43

standing here, I understand how deeply my people's loss of freedom runs, that we are far from the liberation I thought we won the day Syd loosed us from the power of the Black Souls.

"You have a lot of old preconceptions and teachings to work through," Demetrius says in a soft, kind voice, as though seeing into my stunned and confused mind. "But I believe Sage is right, Charlotte."

"Except," I gasp, clinging to the old ways though I wish I didn't, "Sage is a wolf now, and can't turn back to human. If I take the same path, risk this shift, I'll be trapped like him."

The small sorcerer opens his mouth, closes it. Vindication burns with regret. Before I can quit, run and hide from all the years of teachings that beg me to never consider such madness again, Demetrius turns to Sage and offers his hand.

"If you would allow," he says. "I'd like to see why that is."

Even as I gape and struggle with the ingrained werelore controlling my fear, Sage goes to Demetrius immediately, placing his muzzle in the man's hand.

Please, my love says.

I stand there, frozen and aching, as the wolf I love is engulfed in darkness, Demetrius's sorcery licking over him like the vines of a starving plant. If I could move I would go to him, pull him free of the sorcerer, but I can't make my muscles respond, instead staring, eyes tearing as the pair stand there in silence, linked by magic.

Nothing happens for a long moment, except the swish of a silver tail as Sassafras begins to purr. Demetrius grins at the cat, nodding to him as a touch of demon fire whisks over the black. Shenka reaches out with the family magic moments later, blue flames dancing in time with the amber, the darkness not so much absorbing the two as welcoming them. And then I understand. We are made of demon magic and witch. And sorcery.

And the three together might make a miracle happen.

Sage's fur shudders, the white crescent glowing a moment before he whimpers. This time I can move, the instinctual lunge for him born from my need to protect him. But Demetrius is already stepping away, the power of the three dissipating, while Sage shakes himself, panting.

Blue eyes meet mine, smiling. "Now, my dear," Demetrius says. "See what you can see."

I reach for Sage immediately, hope making my heart skip a beat. Is it possible this can be reversed, that my love can take human form again? I will throw aside everything I ever thought I knew if only I can have him back again.

What I feel when I touch Sage's power rocks me back on my heels even as his body shifts and changes, forepaws lifting from the ground, fur shrinking back from him.

He is powerful. So powerful I can hardly comprehend him. And he is truly perfect.

By the time he's done, standing before me in human form, I'm crying, weeping openly, hands covering my mouth as I try to keep from sobbing. His magic is so beautiful, his wolf the most amazing thing I've ever felt. I'm in awe, breaking down in front of all of them. Sage comes to me, green eyes glowing a little, strong hands grasping my upper arms as he pulls me to his naked chest and cradles me there.

Charlie, he sends, voice strong in my head. *It's really going to be okay.*

"I believe Tallah was correct," Demetrius's soft voice interrupts. "Sage is, somehow, the final incarnation to what werewolves can evolve. Rupe's experimentation succeeded where the Black Souls failed." The sorcerer shrugged. "Possibly on purpose. After all, we're looking at the worst fear those evil magickers could ever have conceived."

I glance up, see Shenka is blushing, holding out her robe to Sage, her thin tank top and pajama bottoms revealed. He smiles at her, covers up in the fluffy pink terrycloth while I stay close to him, wiping tears from my face, running my fingers through his dark hair. It's been somehow restored from the horrible bleach job I gave him, as soft and rich in color as ever.

"Of course," Ethpeal says. "The Black Souls knew they created an immense new power. All the controls in the world would never have saved them if the weres had figured out how to evolve on their own."

Demetrius nods. "Exactly, my love," he says, still smiling gently at Sage and me. "And even more so, if the werewolves had been permitted to find their true form—to become full wolves—they surely would have worked it out."

"So we don't lose our humanity," I whisper.

"No, my dear," Demetrius says. "Though it seems the sorcery will lock you in wolf form the first time until you're freed of sorcery by one strong enough to do so."

I weep for all the wolves lost to us because we believed full form meant they were animals. It happened rarely, but enough, by accident or out of grief, weres sometimes retreated to the body of the animal to escape the life we were forced to endure. Now I know the full extent of the lie and can only feel grief for those who thought relief awaited them, to be trapped in a wolf's form with a human's mind forever.

I wish the Black Souls still lived. I would make sure they suffered as much as my people for this.

"It's time to talk to those who need to back the hell off." Sassafras's tail twitches. "Namely, the Enforcers."

"Agreed," Ethpeal says, voice snapping with

irritation. "I'll deal with them myself if I have to."

I laugh out loud, euphoria taking over a moment as I wipe tears from my face. So much has happened, so many revelations, I'm a wreck. But this swing to happy is preferable to the tears I shed for my people. Sage smiles at me, kisses me softly. I touch his face, run my fingers over the scar on his shoulder. "That won't be necessary," I say. "Sage and I will go talk to Erica personally. And then we go home and put an end to the slavery of my people once and for all."

I feel the snap of the shields around the house, tense as Shenka flares with blue fire. My hope for the future is forgotten at the intrusion. Quaid rushes for the stairs to head off the invader, but we all hear the footsteps running through the house, the pounding of them moving down the stairs so fast he doesn't have time to act. I stare in shock as my father staggers the last step, falling into Quaid's arms.

"Raoul." Ethpeal approaches him, touches his arm. My father straightens, dark eyes full of anxiety. I'm surprised to see him. I haven't heard a word from him in a very long time, not since his decision to leave the pack and wander on his own. He ignores Ethpeal, pushing free of Quaid, before turning on me as the family magic flutters around him. It must have let him in because he's my blood, but it's unsure of him, as much as I am.

"What are you doing here?" Ever since my father

abandoned his duty to Syd, he'd chosen to live a lone wolf, outside of the pack. Which means he's no longer eligible to take the throne. I still feel bitterness toward him for his second failure to fulfill his duty, so my tone is sharper than perhaps it should be. But I've been through a great deal and I'm in no mood to coddle him.

"Charlotte." He grasps my arms where Sage once held me, shaking me a little. My love growls at him as though still a wolf but my father ignores him. "You must return home at once."

I pull free, shaking my head. "You gave up the right to give me orders years ago," I snap.

"You don't understand." His voice holds a wail of despair. "It's not for me I beg you." Fear laces through my stomach as he sags before me, a broken werewolf, long damaged. "Your grandfather is in terrible danger. Cicero Caine has been elected wereking."

SEVEN

He has to bring this to me now, to feel his own weak sense of responsibility when I can't do as he asks. I'm saved from having to humiliate my father when Ethpeal interjects herself, pushing him back and away from me.

"And why," she asks in a cold and terrible voice, "are you here if Oleksander is in such danger?" We all wait for a response, but he simply stares at me, mute and anguished. She turns her back on him when he doesn't answer. "Charlotte," she says, tone low, bitter chill gone from her words, "what do you want us to do?"

Part of me wants to plead "why me?" when she looks at me like that. But before I can allow that shred of fear to rise, I feel the wereprincess I am wake to the occasion. Maybe if my father hadn't come, I would have allowed the scrap of weakness life. But no, I am Oleksander's granddaughter, no matter my father's flaws, and I will not allow Caine to hurt my people further. "Raoul Moreau," I snap, though he does not deserve the name, nor has he ever upheld his own father's honor. "You will return to Ukraine, to the true king's side, and you will protect him with your life until I come for him." Zoe's voice echoes in my head even as I argue with myself. I have to go home. I can't trust this to my worthless father.

But I can't go.

He shakes his head, panic on his face. "I am a disgrace," he says, glancing at Sage a moment with a wince of recognition, before turning back to me. I can only guess Raoul is judging Sage, or is that guilt? But does my father understand what Sage has become? It doesn't matter right now. "I cannot go back."

My hand lashes out, claws extended as the wolf in me reacts. She strikes him across the face, blood spilling over his skin, running to drip from his beard onto his rumpled jacket. I watch the cuts seal even as he turns his head from me. Shame, so much shame, and old anger. This is my father, but I am embarrassed to know him, to call him so. I am a Moreau, but he isn't any longer.

"It is well Mother died when she did," I say, my wolf growling behind my voice. "She would have perished from humiliation had she lived to see what you've become."

Raoul, for I will call him Father no more, lifts his

head and meets my eyes. A spark of rage lives on in him. Good, let it bubble, let the resentment and bitterness give him a spine if he won't grow his own. Too many years serving the Dumonts have made him weak and fearful, I see it now. I clung to my mother's teachings all those years, but he remembered nothing of who he was. How often did he fail me when Andre and his sons used me for sport? Perhaps I'm being unkind, since neither of us had any choices then. But the explosive fury I feel bursts like a rupture in my gut, hate, bitterness and old rage waking though I never knew it existed.

My father was a victim then, but I refused to allow myself to be one. And he might have failed me, himself, all of the werenation, but I won't let him fail again. If I can push him to act in anger, maybe there is hope he will do as I say.

"You are a Moreau," I say, though my wolf sniffs at that title, knowing he doesn't deserve to carry the name. "And your father needs you. Now, bury your fear, coward, and do your damned duty. For once, put others ahead of your miserable self-preservation."

He growls at me, face altering, elongating as his wolf emerges. I meet him with my own, my muzzle feeling hot on my human face.

Raoul backs down, but finally nods. Have I woken his pride or merely hurt him enough he knows I'm his master? The answer doesn't matter, but I almost wish I knew if I could rely on him for the right reasons. "I obey your order, Your Highness," he says. "What would you have me do?"

Can't he think for himself? I will not let pity ruin this moment, or softness give him relief. Raoul is a broken man, shattered by years of torment, as much as the Dumonts tried to break me. I have no idea what was done to him, the scope of his own torture. And yet, here I stand, powerful despite the best Andre could dish out. What is the difference between Raoul and I that he failed so long ago and I remained strong?

"Break our king out of prison," I say. "Raise an army of sympathetic weres if you must, but rescue Oleksander before Caine can harm him."

"It would go better with you at my side." He licks his lips, face returned to normal, as has mine.

"I can't come with you." Nor do I have time to explain the Oracle's orders, or contemplate the sick worry she might be wrong. I'm trusting her as I only trust Syd. Why is that? I can't say for certain, though the burning fire we shared in the back of the stolen SUV still seethes inside me and tells me this choice is the right one, no matter my fears. "You must do this alone, Raoul." I reach out and squeeze his shoulder, anger seeping away. I must reach him on a more emotional level, appeal to his pride and loyalties, whatever remains of them. I think of what Shenka said in the back yard, the word that triggered my own agreement to relent. And though perhaps it's a terrible thing to manipulate the werewolf who fathered me, I will not allow my guilt to hold me back. "For our family's honor."

His eyes flicker to Sage, anger returning. "Your people are more important than some revenant."

This time when I hit him, I don't restrain my anger. Raoul spins sideways as he crashes into the stairs, groaning softly, collapsing under the pressure of my magic. I cross to stand over him, hands fisted at my sides as my wolf howls inside me and my need to crush him almost does the same to me.

"Listen to me," I snarl, "because I will only say this once. You will obey or I will kill you myself." He doesn't comment, doesn't try to shield himself from further blows, just lies there. "I am about to turn werelaw into history, rewrite everything we know about our people. This is bigger than Oleksander, bigger than you. Than me. This is our race I'm fighting for." For the first time, I know I speak truth. This isn't some selfish need to save the man I love. This is for the entire werenation. And I won't let them down ever again.

Raoul pulls himself to his feet, nods. "Understood, Your Highness." He pauses. "I'll do my best."

"You won't be doing it alone." Ethpeal comes forward, tugging on Demetrius's hand, though when his look of surprise fades, she doesn't have to encourage him.

"We're coming with you."

Raoul looks like he wants to protest, but I allow him to feel my power again. "They will be of invaluable assistance," I say. "Listen to their counsel and rescue my grandfather."

Ethpeal hugs me quickly as Raoul turns and heads up the stairs. *We'll make sure he's okay*, she sends. *I promise you.*

Thank you. I hug her back, relief awake and alive. I don't have to go home. I trust Syd's grandmother and her husband, if not my own father. If anyone can save Oleksander, it's them.

I stand at the bottom of the stairs, listening to them exit the back door, feel the pull of sorcery as one or both of the married pair open a tunnel to Ukraine. I turn back to the others as my father leaves with Ethpeal and Demetrius, ready to apologize for my behavior, only to gasp as Shenka runs forward and embraces me.

"I'm sorry," she says. "But I know your grandfather will be okay."

I nod to her, try to smile. "I have to believe it." And if Zoe Helios proves to be wrong, if her little foretelling means the death of my grandfather or the detriment of my people, I will hunt her down and make her pay for her deception. Later. For now, I will trust the bit of magic she left with me and hope the trauma she spoke of doesn't mean the death of someone I love.

Quaid stirs, glances at the stairs. "I hate to break up

the party," he says. "But the longer you stay here, the more dangerous this is."

I nod quickly. "You're right." I take Sage's hand, loving the feeling of his skin on mine. "Though maybe some real clothes might be a better choice for meeting Erica the first time?"

Shenka is so adorable when she blushes, turning to the cardboard boxes behind her while Sassafras's tail swishes.

"Vanity," he sniffs. "I highly doubt she'll care what he's wearing when she has the pair of you arrested."

"You think it's a bad idea?" I crouch to face the silver Persian.

"I didn't say that," he grumbles. "But I know Erica better than most of you. And she's not exactly the perfect person for her particular job." His amber eyes seem old to me, wise, though he still speaks with the voice of a demon boy. "Just be careful. And have an exit strategy."

I nod, stroking his fur, as Shenka crosses and hands Sage some clothes. "Always," I say. "Want to come along for the ride?"

He snorts. "Finally, someone realizes my value. But no." He swishes his tail again. "I'm needed here. You can take care of yourself."

Sassafras's job has always been to watch over the children and I respect him for his choice. "Then stop interfering," I say, swatting his tail.

He bares his teeth at me. "So much for respect." He head-butts my hand. "Please," he whispers. "Be careful."

I stand as he runs up the stairs and leaves us behind, the door whispering closed as he pushes his way through. I turn to find Sage sorting through some jeans while Shenka turns her back, hugging herself and grinning. I wink at her before nodding to Quaid.

He nods back, looking relieved, though I know it's just the kids he worries about, and if push came to shove, Quaid would never let anyone hurt us. "Time to get you two to Harvard."

Someone pounds on the kitchen door the moment he's done speaking.

Someone with Enforcer magic and an unwillingness to take no for an answer.

EIGHT

Quaid's feet pound on the stairs as he rushes up to the kitchen. I want to follow him, to protect him if I can, but Shenka blocks me with magic, dark eyes snapping blue power.

"Let him deal with them," she says. "He might be able to talk them down."

I listen, tense, hand holding Sage's as Shenka returns to rummage further through a cardboard box just out of the reach of the light. A soft blue glow casts her in eerie shadows as her hovering witchlight dances over her head. She joins us a moment later with a final pair of jeans and a t-shirt for Sage. He accepts them with a smile and slips the clothes on while Shenka turns away, blushing again.

Her reaction would be adorable if I weren't so afraid.

Someone steps across the threshold of the kitchen,

the Enforcer power having a hard time breaking through the wards. But I hear Pender's voice and know Quaid will not be able to shield us much longer. My ears strain for actual words, but I hear only the muffled sound of a low argument. First Quaid, then Pender, back again. Sage jerks his t-shirt down over his flat stomach just as two more people cross the family magic and my hackles rise.

I don't have to hear their voices to know they are werewolves. And from the tainted feeling of them, they belong to Caine's pack. I'm not surprised then to make out the deep tone of Roman's voice, nor that of his sister, Viveca. The North American Council must have agreed to include Caine's beta and his sibling in the Enforcer's search.

The next time I see Erica, I'm going to make sure she understands just how unhappy her choice has made me.

The already crowded kitchen above swells with two more bodies of power, witches. I make out Finlay's gravel tone with a start of surprise. That means the second must be Gwendolyn. The pair always work together. Has Femke sent the witch pairing to support the werewolves, or to protect Sage and me? I have no way of knowing, though I hope it's the latter.

I can't kid myself about the European leader's position. She must uphold the law, keep the peace, stay out of the conflicts of other races, even if that means turning us over when I know she doesn't want to.

An argument breaks out above, so loud I wince and turn to Shenka. "We have to get out of here." Footsteps approach the basement door, power pushing ahead of it. Shenka scowls, the family magic rising to lick at her legs in blue flames. I feel the family through her, their willingness to protect us, no matter what that might mean for the Hayle coven.

And though a wash of gratitude that stings my eyes with tears and tightens my throat almost consumes me at their loyalty, I can't allow this to go on.

Pender's voice answers Quaid's angry tone, his words coming clearly through the door at the top of the stairs.

"I'm very sorry," he says. "But there is a formal extradition order for the two werewolves hiding in your basement. And I must obey the law."

Shenka spins on us, pushing against me physically with both hands. "Hide," she hisses as the door opens.

I don't know what she expects. There's nowhere to go. But as Sage and I fade into the shadows, I feel the family embrace us fully, their power cloaking us in magic, and as I reach out to them with my own power, Sage's answers. A bubble of energy swallows us whole, dimming the light in the room and I realize we're being hidden by illusion or some magical means. I'm certain Pender will be able to see right through it, and my mind turns to defense and escape by any means as I try to work out a plan.

Pender descends, black robe flowing around him, Quaid close on his heels. The two werewolves follow after, Viveca sniffing the air, her beautiful face ugly in its hate. Roman's shoulders hunch forward as he ducks to clear the low ceiling, hulking darkness making my skin crawl. Viveca hates me, I can only guess, because she's jealous Caine wants me instead of her. Roman just hates.

I catch a glimpse of Gwen and Finlay as Shenka slams up a wall of power in front of Pender, her fury obvious on her pinched face. I've never seen her so angry before and am actually a little nervous she might take things further than she should.

"How dare you?" Her voice vibrates, not with emotion, but with power as the family answers her, the immensity of the Hayle coven's magic flowing around her in a whirling tornado as they answer her call. "You break coven law, invading territory without cause, after segregating and imprisoning our coven in our own homes for days." She doesn't attack, simply stares with growing scorn at the leader of the Enforcers. "For shame, Pender Tremere."

He shrugs, pushing back his hood. He looks even more tired than he did when I saw him in Arizona, when he almost captured Sage and me. I feel sorry for him, for the pressure he is under, and wonder how far Shenka can push him before he breaks. Because he is due to break. No one can endure the constant control he's been under for so many years and not come to a point where they snap.

"Take it up with the Council Leader," Pender says, not a trace of anger in his voice. "I'm sorry, Shenka, but I have my orders."

"So, lawful or not, you'll follow them?" She snorts in his face, closing the distance between them though keeping the wall up and vibrating with magic. "How typical." She waves in the air between them as though he offends her. "Laws are laws until the Council decides it's time to break them."

He sighs, audible, as the two werewolves prod him from behind.

"They are here," Roman growls.

Pender finally reacts, rage flashing over his face, though when he turns, I realize his heart isn't in this hunt at all. "You touch me again," he snarls in Roman's face, "and I'll tear your heart from your chest and make your sister eat it."

No one speaks. I think we're all too shocked by Pender's sudden reaction. I expected him to crack, but this emotional reaction is unlike him. So, he's on our side, after all. Maybe he can be convinced to stand down if approached the right way.

Gwendolyn clears her throat, her golden hair just catching the light of the bulb as Finlay hulks protectively behind her. "If you would allow," she says. "A quick search will answer the question."

Shenka shakes her head, arms crossing over her chest. "Illegal," she says. "The two you seek aren't even witches, and the pair of you are out of your jurisdiction." Finlay scowls at her, though Gwendolyn nods and ducks her head. "This domain is ruled by coven law, not werewolf. Coven law states clearly," she jabs Pender in the chest with one finger as he turns back to face her, a big risk in my opinion, though he doesn't react to the tiny blow, "no Enforcer may search a coven territory without the permission of the coven leader."

His shoulders sag slightly. "Unless the Enforcers have proof the coven leader has broken the law," he says.

"A coven leader who happens to be absent and can't defend herself." Shenka's anger flares a moment before she regains her composure. "Fine. Where's your proof?" She glares at him, then at Gwen and Finlay, totally ignoring the two werewolves. "I'd like to see it."

Pender doesn't comment, leaving the room silent.

"I can smell them," Viveca snarls.

Shenka raises one eyebrow at her, looking the werewoman up and down as though she offends the Hayle second with her very presence. "And I'm taking your word for it, why?"

Was that a tiny quirk at the corner of Pender's tired mouth?

"We acted on their assurance," he says, with more

energy as he turns to them. "I was assured you had concrete proof the two fugitives were here." He scowls, his own power crackling. Has Shenka given him a doorway he can squeeze out his sense of outrage through?

Sassafras's sarcasm cuts like a knife where he perches at the top of the stairs, watching with glowing eyes. "Tell us you haven't breached coven law on the strength of this creature's sense of smell?"

Pender doesn't comment. But I can tell from the set of his shoulders, the way he's not resisting, but waiting for an answer, he is giving us a chance. Pender knows we are here, I'm certain of it. But he hates this chase as much as we do, is clearly upset by his orders. Why else would he react this way?

A tiny thread of hope weaves its way through me. We might escape this after all.

Viveca growls something under her breath while Roman shifts, turning and sniffing the air himself.

"We found a car outside town," he says, gravel over stone, almost as deep as Finlay, though rougher.

"How interesting," Shenka says as Sassafras trots down the stairs and joins her.

"Indeed," he says. "Cars are so rare around here."

Gwendolyn snorts a laugh, covers it with a cough while Viveca snaps her teeth at Shenka. The second reacts with magic, pushing the werewoman back and into one of the support posts.

"Don't ever," Shenka says. "Ever."

I'm sure the two werewolves are going to attack, Roman's fury clear all over his face. But Viveca, released from the family magic, simply links to her brother's side. Even these two can smell the winds of change blowing against them.

Pender turns to Shenka and bows his head. "You understand," he says, "if the two we seek are here, you must turn them over."

Shenka's shoulders lift, head high. "You are welcome to leave, now," she says. "I advise you to do so before Syd gets home." She glances casually at her wrist. "Any minute now."

Pender bows his head. "We will return with evidence," he says.

Shenka shrugs. "You do that."

The Enforcer leader turns, points at the werewolves. "You two," he says. "Out."

They don't argue, though they don't look happy. Quaid escorts them up the stairs, turning to meet Shenka's eyes before closing the basement door firmly behind him.

Shenka kicks at a box, winces and shakes her foot as Sage and I emerge from the shadows, the family's magic releasing the protective field around us. "Damn it," she says. "They wouldn't have tried this if Syd was home."

"They know she's not?" I rub at my arms, goosebumps rising as the family magic dissipates.

"They arrived shortly after Syd left and surrounded Wilding Springs," Sassafras says, leaping up onto the box to groom his front paw. "Whether by design or accident, I have no idea. But Pender knows if Syd was here, she would have been screaming bloody murder long before now."

I nod. And wish she was here as I feel the last of the visitors leave through the family wards. Quaid's magic reinforces the shielding at the kitchen door, the power rippling through the energy in the basement, before returning to join us. His grim expression makes me nervous all over again.

"They'll be back," he says. "Pender now has solid proof Syd's not home."

Shenka nods, sadness on her face. "I should be stronger," she says.

Quaid shakes his head as I go to her and hug her.

"You," I say, "are perfect."

"You handled them better than I would," Quaid says. "If those two werewolves had taken one more step into the basement, I would have killed the both of them and the law be damned."

"We have to talk to Erica, and we can't wait any longer." Shenka offers her hand. When Sage tries to join us, Shenka waves him off. "You stay here with Quaid and

Sass," she says. "We don't want to hand you over just yet, not until we know what kind of reception we get."

I hate to leave him behind, but I know he's in good hands. Sage hesitates before hugging me, tight and almost desperate. It's nice to feel his human form again, to smell his human scent and feel the softness of his skin and hair as I kiss him gently.

"We'll be back soon," I say, waving to Quaid. "Thank you."

Syd's husband's smile is dark, but that's Quaid. "Be careful."

Shenka's body begins to glow with blue fire and I raise my eyebrows in curiosity.

"Quaid's been teaching me a few things," she says with a wink. "Got a little tired of Syd being the only one who could travel long distance. The Enforcer trick of riding the elemental fire comes in handy at times like this."

I grasp her warm hand and smile. "Seems like the two of us need to have a chat," I say. "Compare notes."

Shenka's dark eyes glitter with fierce joy. "You got it. When this is over."

Blue flames lick at me, reminding me of Zoe Helios and I wonder if the fire she uses for her oracles follows the same rules. And then there is no time for my mind to wander or my wolf to speculate, because the family magic flares around us and we are engulfed.

NINE

I gasp a breath as we flare out of the fire and into the dark Yard at Harvard.

"Thought showing up in her office might piss off Erica," Shenka says, looking around. "It's late enough here hopefully no one saw us arrive." This far into September at Harvard means the students are in session. But I also know how careful Shenka is. And right now, I couldn't care less if some freshman needs their memory wiped.

I cross to Massachusetts Hall at Shenka's side, the familiarity of Harvard and the green space of the Yard tugging at my emotions. I spent years here with Syd, protecting her, watching her stumble and fall, only to pull herself back up again. I missed out on her last year, the bond between us broken, and fled to Ukraine to save my family though I knew it was a trap.

A shiver passes down my spine as we walk over the threshold into the hall and head for the elevator. Shenka's dark expression tells me she's in her own memories. Or, planning what she's going to say to Erica. I should probably stop traveling my own past and focus on the present.

The elevator groans softly as we ride it upward. The soft ding when the doors open on the Council Leader's floor makes me wince. I realize the goal here isn't to sneak up on Erica, but to give her a little warning so we don't freak her out, but I've been tiptoeing around for what seems like forever. Giving up on cloak and dagger for the direct approach feels wrong.

A young man with ginger hair and a face full of freckles greets us as we pass through the main door and into the dark-paneled sitting room. Syd confessed to me this place always made her feel anxious, as though the portraits of the Leaders on the walls were judging her. I have to agree, though for different reasons. My memories of this place include Maurice, Miriam's former secretary and the thief who took Gabriel from Syd. Not to mention the years of suffering Syd endured while her mother was under the control of the Brotherhood.

And now Erica is leader, I feel no better about this room, or the energy in it, though the red-haired witch seems amiable enough. I know him from his days as a page. It seems Phillip has moved up in the world.

"Coven Second Hayle," he says with a little bow for Shenka. "How can I assist you?"

"I need to see the Council Leader," Shenka says. "Immediately."

He nods, turning toward the door to the office, though his eyes seem troubled. "You do know I have to call the Enforcers?" Phillip's gaze flickers to me and back again.

"If you could hold off on that," she says. "Clearing up this mess is the reason we're here."

He hesitates before nodding with a smile. "I will leave it up to the Leader to decide," he says, turning his little grin to me. "I wish you both well this evening."

I have no idea if we can trust him, but he feels and smells as though he's relaxed, calm, and I sense no deceit in him. Regardless, we're about to walk into the dragon's den, so a few Enforcers at the door will hardly make a difference if Phillip is going to summon them.

Shenka leads the way. I feel tense and ready for a fight as I follow her. I catch a glimpse of Erica behind her desk as I close the door, turning to stand at Shenka's side when the Council Leader looks up. Her blonde bob shifts against her cheek, blue eyes tight around the edges, hands clenching as she sets down her pen and sits back. She doesn't seem surprised to see us, so I know either Shenka has warned her of our arrival or Pender has updated her on his visit to the house.

"Shenka." Erica doesn't bother with titles, her voice tight and angry. "I take it Syd still isn't back?"

To Shenka's credit, she doesn't flinch. "I've come to appeal to you, Council Leader. On behalf of two who are being falsely persecuted."

Erica turns to me, expression still flat and angry. "You took a big risk coming here, Charlotte," she says. "And while I'm not unsympathetic to your plight, I have a job to do."

I nod. I've never warmed to this woman, though I know she truly cares for the coven she left, for Syd and the family. For that reason alone, I'm willing to plead my case to her.

"I am well aware you are being pressured to turn me over to the werenation," I say. "But the reason for my arrest is no longer an issue."

She raises her carefully shaped eyebrows. The act makes her look older, less like the woman I know and more like a caricature of the Leader she's become.

"He's dead, then?" So callous. I would never have expected such lack of empathy from her. The coldness of her reaction makes my wolf chuff in anger.

"Alive and well," Shenka says. "More than well. That's our point." She forms a hologram out of magic, showing Erica Sage's transformation, the feeling of him so powerful in the room it's as though he's here with me.

That brings me comfort as Shenka goes on. "Whatever the origins of Sage America's infection, he has not devolved into revenant darkness. Instead, he has developed into a power beyond that which the werewolves themselves possess."

Erica doesn't seem impressed, waving off Shenka's magic, though her anger seems to fade some as she sighs and presses both hands firmly down on the desktop.

"That's a matter for the werenation," she says. "Not for this Council. No matter what he's become, he must be returned to Ukraine to face the werewolves."

"We would like to request your support in presenting his case." Shenka gestures to me. "If the North American Council is willing to stand with Charlotte and Sage, it could offer not only weight to his case, but go a long way to ensuring he receives a fair trial on the other end."

I already know what Erica is going to say before she says it. The room suddenly stinks of fear and desperation, and I wonder if she is cracking under the pressure of this office.

"You have no idea the amount of leeway I'm giving you, just allowing you to stand here," Erica snaps. "I am being lobbied heavily both by the werenation and the Steam Union to return the both of you to Europe immediately." But not the European Council? That's interesting information. Femke is staying out of it, then? Why the visit from Gwendolyn and Finlay, if so?

"We understand that," Shenka says in her best soothing tone while my mind chatters on, but Erica stands, shaking her head, magic crackling around her.

"You don't," she says. "I'm sorry, I really am. I feel for you, Charlotte, for this mess you're in. But you've dragged too many coven families—not to mention forcing a young sorcerer to defect from the Steam Union—for me to allow this to go on." Two families, I almost correct her, covens who aren't fans of the Council in the first place. And it was Piers's decision to leave his mother's oppressive rule, with no urging from me. But I allow this pathetic woman her accusations while planning, yet again, the best escape routes from the room.

Sassafras was right to counsel caution, as I knew he would be.

"Council Leader," Shenka says, but Erica cuts her off.

"The law is the law," she says. "And while we might not agree with the rules of other cultures, we must uphold them, Shenka." Erica's face twists a moment, a hint of her fear showing. "There must be order or all of this," she waves around the room, "all of what we've built, is for nothing." She turns to me, hopelessness in her eyes. "I know you feel like I'm betraying you. But if you're right, if this young man isn't a danger to your people, I'm sure justice will prevail and he will be exonerated."

Except that Caine is on the throne. And will be perfectly willing to kill Sage or use him as a pawn if he is able to capture him. There is no justice waiting for me or for Sage in Ukraine. Only death.

I shrug, refusing to give her any relief from the guilt I hope is eating her. "Thanks for nothing," I say.

Shenka's sadness only shows a moment. "Very well," she says. "Thank you for your time. We'll be going."

Erica laughs, humorless and cold. "You really think I'm that stupid, to let you two go?" Her power flares, her voice echoing as Pender's face appears in glowing blue. "Enforcer Leader Tremere," Erica says in a voice that crackles with power. "You will enter the Hayle house and remove the fugitive."

His face is flat and expressionless, voice as chilly as hers. "I have no solid proof of his presence," Pender says. "You wish me to break coven law to conduct a search?"

Erica's anger surges across her whole body, though I smell the fear behind it. She is so afraid to fail, she is becoming the kind of leader the Council doesn't need.

"You have your orders," she snaps. "Obey them immediately."

She turns on us as Pender's image sizzles out.

"I will have the two of you out of my territory," she says. "And until this is resolved, Charlotte, you will not be welcome back here. If then."

I open my mouth to tell her exactly where she can shove herself while Enforcer magic approaches from beyond the door. We're cornered, and I doubt highly

Shenka will be able to get us out of here past all the magic wards.

I'm sorry, Shenka sends. *This is my fault. We should have gone to Femke.*

I tense, prepared to fight. And I will fight, heart aching, knowing the Enforcers are now entering Syd's house, putting her children at risk, that they will find Sage. Erica snaps her fingers and the door opens, time slows down. I won't be taken. I have to find a way to escape so I can make this right.

I half-turn toward the opening door, the three tall Enforcers raising their hands toward me, glowing blue fire at the ready, just as the air beside me tears wide and a furious woman with dark hair and rainbow magic strides through.

TEN

Syd has never been one to hide how she feels, but from the fury on her face, I can tell she's angrier than I've ever seen her. Erica backs off two hurried steps as the door behind me slams shut in the Enforcer's faces. I hear them pounding on the door, their magic buffering against Syd's while she stalks forward, totally silent for once, teeth bared, hands fisted at her sides.

Erica retreats behind her desk, shaking, eyes huge, hands up in front of her as the power of the Council holds off Syd. "How dare you barge in here," Erica splutters.

Syd laughs. It's not a pretty sound and I back her up by spinning past Shenka and flanking the Council Leader, keeping her pinned behind her desk, cutting off her chance of retreat. Syd ignores me, one hand rising, index finger on fire as she jabs it into Erica's chest so hard the woman jerks back.

"You," she says in a deathly quiet voice, "will call off your Enforcers right now," Syd pokes her again, smoke rising from the front of Erica's shirt, "and get them the hell out of my house," her voice rises, louder, full of power as she grows a few inches, towering over Erica, rainbow magic in flames around her, "or I will make sure you never see the light of day again."

Shenka holds her place, but she interrupts the silence that falls after a few heartbeats.

"Coven Leader," she says. "Nice of you to join us."

"I was busy," Syd says, eyes still locked on Erica. "Sorry to take so long."

"Not at all." Shenka shifts her weight to one foot, an amused expression warming her face. "Though your timing is, as always, impeccable."

Syd shrinks to her normal size and for the first time I really see why Shenka is her perfect choice for second. I love Syd, she is a sister of my heart, but her temper and the power she holds make her borderline uncontrollable, pushing her past her empathy to the edge of uncaring. Shenka's easy manner and ability to diffuse any situation makes her invaluable. While Syd's fury is legendary—and, in this case, justified—killing the Council Leader would likely put her on the fugitive list, too.

Erica seems to sense the shift in mood and her terror

fades in favor of indignation. "How dare you threaten me."

"I mean it, Erica," Syd says, turning her back on the Council Leader. "Don't screw with me. You'll lose and you know it. Get your Enforcers out of my territory now, or I'll report you to the World Councils. And we'll see how well that goes over, a Council Leader blatantly breaking coven law."

Erica's face falls, twists into desperation. "I had no choice."

"You always have a choice." Syd sounds tired, meets my eyes. "Hey, Charlotte." She gestures at the two of us. "Let's go home and make sure the kids are still asleep." She spins to glare at Erica. "You better hope those jackasses didn't wake my children, or I'll be back."

"You can't take her." Erica's show of bravery is a surprise, even to Syd.

"Considering," Syd snaps as she takes my hand, Shenka's in her free one, "this isn't a North American problem, that you are, for some reason only known to you, turning another race's issues into your own, I can do whatever the hell I want." Syd's magic flares around us. "Word of advice from here on in, Erica. Mind your own damned business."

I feel the veil, now familiar to my own magic, as Syd tears it open and pulls us through. Before the seam seals shut, I hear Erica screaming after us.

"Sydlynn Hayle! You won't get away with challenging the law forever!"

Her words echo in the dark, dying at last as we step out the other side. I stumble as we do, expecting the cold basement in Wilding Springs, shock sending shivers through me as I stare across a second desk into Femke Svennson's surprised face. She's clearly in the dark about this visit as I am, though Syd doesn't allow for hesitation.

"Femke," she says, leaning forward with her fists on the Council Leader's desk. "We have to talk."

Femke stands quickly, gesturing at the door behind us as the feeling of even more Enforcers crests against it. But this Council Leader isn't desperate or afraid. Instead, she circles the desk to hug me tight, her crisp scent making me sad.

"Charlotte," she whispers in my ear. "I'm so happy you're all right."

She releases me, goes to the door as Syd grabs me this time, hugs me close.

"In case you were wondering," she grins, voice dry as she pulls away, "we were all worried about you."

I blink away some tears, knowing my proximity to her is making me even more emotional. "I know," I say.

"Sage is okay?" Syd takes a seat, kindly ignoring my rising tears, Shenka patting my shoulder before joining her in another. I slide to the cushion of the last as Femke finishes her whispered conversation through a crack in the door before joining us. She sits on the front of her desk, arms crossed over her chest, as she looks around at the three of us, taking in Shenka's pajamas, Syd's rumpled t-shirt and dirty jeans. I glance at the clock on the desk, remembering it's five hours ahead here, and accept the glow of dawn lighting in the east with weary recognition.

"I take it there's a story I need to hear." Femke rises again, goes to the side of the room, pouring hot coffee from a carafe. I join her, helping pass out steaming mugs while Syd sighs happily and accepts hers.

"Just another day at the office," she says, blue eyes sparkling.

I sit next to her, worry clenching my hands around the hot mug. "The house?" I can't meet her eyes, guilt stinging. I've put the family in so much danger.

"Mom's there," Syd says, all casual as she sips her coffee. "And Max and a couple of his closest friends." The drach. They will not allow anything bad to happen to the coven. I breathe a sigh of relief and finally turn my head to look at her. She leans in and touches my cheek, fingers heated from her coffee mug. "It's covered. And Sage is safe. I promise. Erica won't dare go near him now."

I nod, too choked up to answer, or to tell her it wasn't Sage I was worried about, but the kids. I should have known Syd would never leave them unprotected.

Femke's eyes are curious behind the rim of her mug.

"Trouble with my counterpart?"

I sink into the chair, resting the mug in my lap, the scent of coffee perking me almost as much as drinking it. "I have a lot to tell you."

It takes about an hour. By the time I'm done, the sun is up, the sky bright outside Femke's window. I stare out into the new day, watch students begin to trickle about the campus, the view of the main concourse almost hypnotic as life goes on, normal life, beyond this room.

When I'm finally done, Syd sets her mug down on Femke's desk. "We have to see Sage," she says.

Femke nods. "I need to examine him, Charlotte. To prove to myself he's what you say he is."

Even now, I hesitate, though these are my friends and I know Syd would never put us in danger.

I'll be there, she sends, voice strong and familiar in my head. *If Femke starts talking turning him over to the werewolves, I'll take you to Meems. You'll be safe on Demonicon.*

I reach out and squeeze her hand. *Thank you*, I send. *But you put the family first.*

Syd's mind hugs mine. *You are family*, she sends before she stands and nods to Femke. I join her, meeting the Council Leader's eyes, opening my magic to her on impulse. I reach for her with my power and Femke kindly reaches back. I feel her concern, her strength and her absolute faith in me.

"I promise you," Femke says. "I won't make any

decisions without talking it over first. All right?"

I hug her. I seem to have become rather demonstrative lately. Femke doesn't seem to mind. And honestly, neither do I.

ELEVEN

I step out beside Syd into the basement at Wilding Springs to a larger crowd of magic beings than I was expecting. Sage rushes forward to hug me while a dozen drach hover in the background, Max standing with Quaid and Miriam, Shenka staying out of the way. I hug my love, welcome his kiss, grateful my friends give me a moment to share a quiet reunion with him.

It's going to be okay, he sends. *I already talked to Max.* His mind shivers while his body responds in kind. *He's one of the dragon things, isn't he? Same smell.*

I nod against his shoulder. *He's the leader of the drach*, I say. *And Syd's good friend.*

The Enforcers came back, Sage sends. *But Max and Syd's mom sent them packing.*

I would have paid good money to see that confrontation. *Femke needs to examine you*, I send, gesturing to the tall blonde. Sage turns, his arm around my shoulders, to extend his hand to the Council Leader. She shakes it without hesitation as Sage speaks.

"Whatever you need to prove I'm not a threat," he says. "I'm all yours."

"Did they get in?" Syd's pissed all over again, Quaid embracing her before shrugging.

"Briefly," he says. "Very briefly."

Max inclines his big head to Syd as she turns to him, still in Quaid's arms.

"I ensured they would wait outside for you," the drach leader says. "Their leader seemed most congenial when I assured him I would not allow him or his people to remain inside your home." He speaks softly, with a smile in his voice, but I've seen Max in full drach form and know very well how frightening he and his people can be.

"I think Pender was impressed." Miriam's smile is dark, arms crossed elegantly over her chest, beautiful face in shadow, reminding me of a wicked witch from a fairy tale. Sometimes I forget how truly powerful and frightening these people can be when they are crossed.

Syd's anger isn't diminished despite Max's assistance. She scowls at her mother before shrugging. "Excuse me," she grumbles to everyone in general. "I have some

Enforcer asses to kick out of Wilding Springs."

She leaves, stomping up the stairs with her mother at her side, Max and his drach filing after her. The stairs groan under the weight of their feet, a column of gray-clad, diamond-eyed creatures I wouldn't want to cross. I feel the coven gathering around the house above ground and can only guess they've managed to hold off the Enforcers, not drive them away. Max is too much a diplomatic soul to do anyone any real harm. I'm sure he was happy to help, but the end game has to be Syd's.

There will be a great deal of magic thrown around tonight, I would imagine, and a lot of covering up to do, but it's nothing this town isn't used to. Thankfully, the residual magic left behind by the Sidhe Gate still suppresses the interest of the townsfolk in anything to do with magic. Still, something this huge can't go unnoticed.

I should go help Syd, but I can't bring myself to leave Sage while Femke pulls him into a quiet corner and her power engulfs him, without warning. Sassafras paws my leg, so I bend and pick him up, cuddling him to me, the scent of his white fur in my nose as he speaks in my head.

You must have pissed off Erica pretty bad, he sends. *She threw everything she had at us.*

I'm sorry. I stroke his tail, cradling him in the crook of one arm, but he bats at my nose, amber eyes sparkling.

Silly, he sends. *Pissing off Erica to the point she breaks is an art. Good job.*

I laugh. I can't help it, though it's a quiet, subdued sound. *Thanks, Sass.*

Syd arrived just as you two left, he sends. *We managed to fill her in before she lost her crap.* He chuckles softly. *There was a time I worried about her. Still do. That temper of hers is going to get her into more trouble than she can handle one of these days.*

But not today. I hug him, kiss his forehead.

The whole world seems to shudder, a giant boom echoing from the world above. I feel the house shift slightly to the left, held in place by the family magic and Shenka's hurried reaction. Total silence falls overhead as Quaid scowls and shakes his head.

"She better not wake the kids," he says, echoing her warning to Erica.

More laughter, this time from Shenka, Sass and I. Even Femke emerges from the blue flames to grin at him while Quaid grins back. The kitchen door slams as the pressure of power around the house eases and leaves. When Syd returns, she has only her mother and Max with her.

"Babe," Quaid says, all casual. "All set?"

"They won't be back," she snaps. "Ever."

Shenka gasps, but Miriam laughs, her lovely amusement lightening the mood further.

"What my darling daughter means," Miriam says, "is Pender has seen the error of his ways and has taken his Enforcers—and the werewolves seeking you—

elsewhere."

I cock my head to the side, curiosity burning. "Why?"

Syd shrugs, grumpy and rumpled as Quaid spins her around and hugs her from behind, resting his chin on the top of her head.

"He values coven law more than his orders," Syd says.

"Especially when that coven law is reinforced by the holographic support of three World Council Leaders." Miriam shakes out her dark hair, smiling in satisfaction. "Nice call. I raised you well, sweetheart."

Syd wrinkles her nose at her mother before grinning suddenly like she's found the funny in the whole thing. "Thanks, Mom." Her eyes shift to Femke who steps back from Sage. My love shakes his head, hands on his temples, Femke's fingers brushing apologetically over his cheek. She turns to us, a frown on her face.

"He feels clean," she says. And sighs. "But I have nothing to compare him to, Charlotte. The stumbling block for me is he doesn't feel like a real werewolf, like you. And while he feels nothing like a revenant, we both know he has to be above reproach if you are going to convince the werenation he's safe." She drops her hands to her sides with an apologetic sigh. "We both know there is nothing empty or soulless about Sage. But any hint of difference could be used against his case as reason to have him killed, simply from the old, ingrained fears of your race."

I understand what she's saying. "He's not a revenant, but unless we can prove he's a real werewolf, the law can be manipulated."

She nods. "I fear that's the case."

Sage comes to my side. I set Sassafras on the ground and take Sage's offered hand, his face sad, sea-green eyes full of love for me. "We can't run forever, Charlie. Maybe we need to face this down and take our chances."

I bite my lower lip while Syd's mind touches mine.

Demonicon waits, she sends.

But I can't live like that, as a creature on another plane. Sage is right. We have to try, at least. With Syd as a last resort. I touch his face, feel his wolf—feel him—all one entity. And hear mine chuff softly in regret.

The moment the memory of his suggestion crosses my mind, I shudder from it, only to pull myself back. As I stare into Sage's eyes, the repulsion of the plan fades, strengthening in conviction, until my heart is pounding with the need to see if it will work.

I turn to Femke as concern crosses my love's face, his hands reaching for me. "You said you have nothing to compare him to," I say. "What if you did?"

Sage doesn't speak, or argue, as Femke frowns at me. "I don't understand."

I spread my hands in front of me, looking down at them, picturing paws. Real paws, not the wereclaws I'm used to, but the slim shape of a wolf's. "We are taught allowing ourselves to shift to full wolf form is dangerous," I say. "That we will lose our humanity to the form, become true wolves, lost to the creature we carry within. I've never done so before, for that reason."

Femke nods. "It's in the file," she says, flushing a little. Her and her precious files. It makes me wonder what else she knows about us, but there will be time to investigate later.

"If I've learned anything from this experience," I say, "it's that everything has changed." I meet Syd's worried eyes. "Since you freed us, we've been following the same laws, the same rules that governed us from the beginning. But we are more than the Black Souls made us. We have moved past the controls they placed on werewolves. We are no longer restricted to the ways of our teachings. And Sage is proof of that."

No one speaks as I step back, pulling at my t-shirt, reaching for my wolf. "I've felt all along, since I gained control of my magic, something is missing." My wolf chuffs at me, sounding eager, and I welcome her agreement. "That a final block holds me back from fully attaining my potential, the last of the controls not, perhaps, created by power, but by superstition and corrupted belief." My t-shirt hits the floor, body already morphing toward wereshape. My claws make short work of the zipper on my jeans, the fabric falling to the concrete as my legs shift, back hinged, paws slipping out of my shoes. I step out onto the basement floor, inside the pentagram, in my underwear and blonde fur, though I know the last of my clothing, too, will fall free of me if I succeed. "And I believe that block comes from my failure to embrace my true shape. It's time to find out if the Black Souls lied about this, as they did everything else."

"Charlotte." Syd's voice is full of concern, but she doesn't try to stop me. "Are you sure?"

I nod, my ears perking forward as the wolf in me waits calmly for me to act, fear vanishing as I meet Sage's eyes and finally let go of the teachings holding me back. "I've never been so sure of anything."

TWELVE

I turn within, feeling Sage's steady presence beside me. He's already shifting, his own clothes discarded, body melting from human to wolf so fluidly jealous pangs trouble me. Now, more than ever, I believe he is what I'm meant to be. I've spent the last week and a half fearful he would become something to revile and despise, only to be shocked by his final transformation and the perfection of his power.

His magic hovers beside me, not intruding, but firm and ready to support me if I need it. The others back away, watching, Sassafras's tail beating a steady time as he glares with a cat's intensity. Syd is doing her best to hide her worry. The only person who seems calm is Max. He watches with his diamond eyes as I allow my wolf to take me to wereform.

This is familiar, the feel of my hybrid shape, the bend of my back legs and the thick fur on my body. My bones ache a brief moment as they always do from the shift in their configuration, but the pain is gone as quickly as it comes. I lick my chops in a nervous reaction, though my wolf feels relaxed. I embrace her with power and show her what I want her to do, the image of a blonde wolf coming easily to me. She isn't remotely surprised and, in fact, reacts with amusement I seem to feel the need to address her directly.

She answers with a surge of power before I can change my mind, diving headlong into the magic that makes me what I am. For a moment, I'm running through a fragrant forest, the wind in my fur, crushing leaves under my paws, and then I'm back here in Syd's basement, a sharp jerk of agony making me whimper.

And then, I'm looking up at Syd's shocked face, my body in perfect balance beneath me. Even so, when I try to take a step, I collapse to my haunches with a startled yip at how odd it feels to be on all fours. A quick look down and my sharp eyes—at least ten times more so than when I'm in wereform—catch the minute cracks in the concrete under the pads of my paws. A rush of smells assaults me suddenly as I fully integrate, overpowering with a mix of lilacs and chocolate and dust, of magic and ancient power that has to be Max. I backpedal a few steps, feeling the fur on my ruff rise, my tail sweeping between my back legs as I struggle to adapt.

I'm a wolf, a woman no longer. Even as fear tries to take over, I settle into calm, the steady logic of my true form soothing, welcoming me to embrace it. The last of my anxiety is gone as I fully open to the creature I have always been meant to become. And find a massive well of magic energy open like a blooming flower inside me.

That, I wasn't expecting.

I was strong before, able to tap into the power Syd freed. But the feeling I always had, how something more waited for me, is long gone. Finally, at long last, nothing stands between me and the power I was born with. This shape has freed me from the remains of the controls of the Black Souls.

His scent turns my head, tart with pheromones and familiarity. Sage stands next to me, shoulder a few inches above mine, the white crescent feeding into the faint glow around him. His green eyes flare with magic as he circles me, panting softly, nudging me with his nose.

He smells… delicious and captivating. I want to rub my full body length against him, his need as powerful as mine. I whine like a puppy, barking softly my passion for him as he nuzzles my throat with his powerful jaws.

Someone clears their throat, the vibration of the sound breaking my attention on Sage. If I were a woman, I would blush at the show of affection we just shared, at my need to be with him in this form, the animal passion driving me to mate with him. But I am a wolf at last, and such things are natural to me.

I leave him, padding across the floor to snuffle at Sassafras. The silver Persian bats softly at my nose in response.

"Dog breath," he says.

I bark once, a laugh, sitting on my haunches, the cool of the concrete slowly making its way through my fur. Syd crouches next to me, Femke on my other side as the rest of my friends gather around and Sage comes to join me.

Syd's fingers slide hesitantly through my fur and I sweep my tongue over her cheek in a surge of joy. She laughs, wiping at the trail of saliva before grinning at Femke.

"Well?" Syd's eyes are bright, full of challenge. I can feel both their magicks investigating and remain as open as I can, my power locked with Sage's as he links with me.

"Well." Femke smiles at last, shaking her head, a bit of awe in her voice. How odd their words sound in this form, layered with so many notes, and full of meanings I'm certain aren't meant to be ascertained. I must explore the world around me in this shape, to see what wonders I've been missing by holding back for so long. "My apologies, Sage," Femke says to my love. "I had to be certain. And now, I am." She stands, crossing her arms over her chest, her own faint glow the blue of witch magic. "I would offer the support of the European Witches Council to both of you."

I yip a bark of joy while Sage leans happily against me and moans a soft thanks.

Something shakes the house so violently, I'm on my feet, snarling and snapping the air while Sage's ears flatten, body slinking low to the ground. Syd swears and turns, running for the stairs, her mother on her heels. I try to follow, but Femke's magic holds me back.

"One last thing," she says. "Prove to me you can both reverse the process and I'll do everything in my power to ensure your safety, including confronting a fellow Council Leader in her own territory."

I know what a huge offer she's making and why she's making it. The touch of Erica's power is so clear I can taste it, even through all the wards around Syd's house. The Council Leader herself has come to confront us and take us away.

The thought rises Femke could simply whisk Sage and I back to Oxford with her. But she's suggesting she take our case to the other who hunts us, to speak on our behalf and hopefully assure our safe passage if we ever return to North America. I nod, though I don't wish to become human again, not yet. Being a wolf is so much better, cleaner, the feeling of it the most natural I've ever encountered.

Longing to remain in wolf form switches on my

natural suspicion and shakes my calm.

Is this the danger of becoming full wolf? Not the loss of humanity at all, but the massive power and pull to remain in my intended form? Perhaps. And yet, I can't help but doubt that's the case as I focus and retreat from the wolf I am and into the woman's body I've worn for so long. Shenka rushes forward with my clothing, eyes firmly on me and not on Sage while I wink at her, suddenly filled with joy and feeling giddy knowing, regardless my wants, I'm in control. For the first time, there are no constraints on me aside from the needs of my heart.

The power. It's still there. I feared I could only access it while a wolf. But it lives in all my forms now, awakened and unable to be contained. I am whole at last.

Femke drops her folded arms and nods to me, beaming a smile as a massive boom overhead tells me Syd isn't taking crap from whoever has come to call. The European leader offers her hand to me, the other to Sage and together we climb the stairs to the kitchen. Sassafras scampers ahead of us, Shenka and Max following with Quaid taking the tail. I feel him leave us, heading for the hall and the stairs, and know he's gone to check on the kids.

I don't wait for Femke's urging, aiming for the kitchen door and the driveway. Bright blue light flares as I step out onto the asphalt, looking up at the ring of

Enforcers hovering in the air, the center of their half circle taken by the furious and crackling form of Erica Plower.

When her blue eyes fix on me, she snarls in fury, though that snarl dies away when she realizes Femke is with us.

"Council Leader Plower." Femke nods casually to her, pleasant tone belying the tense situation. Syd's rainbow power crackles as she steps back and allows the European leader some space. But I can tell from my friend's expression, if Erica pushes her any further, Syd will push back and not with happy consequences.

The Enforcers hover closer, and I realize why as I scan the sky behind them. Max stands behind Syd, glittering eyes focused on Erica, but his drach are watching from above, hovering in the dark sky in a triangle formation of watchful patience, though they have yet to engage. Miriam's grim expression can only mean she's convinced Syd to trust diplomacy at this point.

Erica's jaw tightens visibly as she settles to the ground, gesturing for her threatening posse to join her. I spot Pender's troubled face behind her as he does as ordered.

"What are you doing here, Femke?" Erica's tone is sharp, piercing.

"Collecting a pair of long-lost residents of my territory," the European leader says with a smile. "I'm grateful for your concern, but North American assistance is no longer required." She shrugs. "Happy to take them off your hands."

For a moment, Erica looks like she's going to argue and I can only wonder why. Isn't the whole point of her pursuit to turn us over to the authorities? It makes me anxious she has other ideas in mind for Sage and me. Surely, she wouldn't care either way on her own.

Who is it, then, making Erica so nervous about letting us go?

A pair of werewolves slink into the light and I curse myself for not paying closer attention. Of course, she's been speaking with Roman and Viveca. Still, what could they possibly have over the Council Leader to make her argue against our removal?

When she spots the Knox siblings, Erica almost looks relieved and I wonder if I'm imagining things after all. She gestures at Sage and me with a disdainful expression.

"Fine," she says. "Get them out of my territory. I've had enough trouble over this as it is." She glares at Syd. "You and I will have a conversation about your actions, Coven Leader."

"And yours, Council Leader," Syd snaps back. "And yours."

"They are to be turned over to us." Roman's voice is a deep grunt of dissatisfaction as his sister snarls silently at me.

"Take it up with the Europeans," Erica snaps at him before rising into the air. Her Enforcers join her, two in the back remaining behind as I recognize the slim shape of Gwendolyn and that of her hulking companion, Finlay. I had hoped Pender would be relieved by this change of events, but when he meets my eyes, his are troubled. I must think to pursue this further. Something isn't right with the Council.

The Knox siblings glare in rage as Erica and her people leave. Femke snaps her fingers, the air around us turning blue. Gwendolyn and Finlay hurry forward, flanking us. But when Syd moves to join us, Femke shakes her head.

"They belong to the werenation." This time Viveca speaks, her hateful eyes locked on me, claws extending as she partially shifts.

"New information on their status has come to light," Femke says in her crisp, precise way, cutting the werewolves off. "I have a great deal to discuss with Wereking Oleksander." I know she's chosen her words carefully, that she's aware of my grandfather's fall from grace.

"You'll find a new king on the throne," Roman says, his sister smirking her angry glee.

"We shall see if he's able to maintain his position for long," Femke says, taking a step toward them, still encased in the blue fire she's raised. "You might want to tell your 'king', the werenation exists at the discretion of the Witch Council. We have allowed your people autonomy to this point. Were circumstances to change, circumstances which make the Council unhappy, we would have to take steps to ensure the safety and protection of the werenation, even if that means imposing our own laws."

The thought makes me sick to my stomach, but I know it's just a threat. The Knox siblings, however, seem taken aback by her power-backed statement.

Without waiting for them to respond, she turns to Syd. "Thank you for the hospitality," she says. "We'll keep you posted."

I don't have time to say goodbye, only to wave, as the flames of Femke's power flare bright and she carries us off. I draw a deep breath, grateful for the progress we've made. This may be a first step, but it's a big one. And I can finally allow the hope shivering inside me to blossom and grow.

As we step out onto the wooden floor in Femke's office, I briefly wonder about the trauma Zoe mentioned and wonder if I've managed to avoid it. If so, does that mean I can go back to Ukraine?

Only one way to find out.

THIRTEEN

I'm not surprised when Syd appears only a moment later, Max at her side. Femke laughs and hugs her, her greeting wiping the scowl of determination from my friend's face.

Syd grins sheepishly as Femke releases her. "I thought you'd put up a fight."

The European leader shakes her head, patting Syd's cheek. "I know better. Besides, I had to create at least a show of being impartial." She turns to Gwendolyn and Finlay. "Thank you for your service," she says. "Report later."

The pair bow to her before turning to go, though Gwen pauses long enough for a quick embrace before leaving.

I'm focused on another as they close the door behind

them, taking two steps before engulfing Syd in my arms. She hugs me back, lips cool on my cheek. She doesn't let me go for a long moment, mind locking with mine.

One hurdle down, she sends. *Just a few more to go. Ready to trot home and rescue your grandfather, crush Caine and his crew, and restore order to the Universe?*

Hell yeah, I send, using one of her favorite sayings. Syd laughs and pulls back, tears glistening in her eyes.

"Just another day at the office," she says.

"You know it." I turn and take Sage's hand while he leans in and kisses Syd's cheek.

"Who knew you were a paranormal rock star," he says.

Syd rolls her eyes, a faint blush on her cheeks. "Smartass."

"I'm sorry to cut short the victory party, but we have something we have to talk about." Femke's serious tone sharpens my worry back to a razor edge. "I'm going to offer Sage a pardon, but that's only in the witch world, you understand?"

We both nod.

"But," Femke says, "if I do that, you realize I'll have to offer the same to Caine and his pack."

I stare at her in shock. "Why?"

Syd sighs and nods, Sage, too.

"Makes sense," he says. "Logical, really. Which must then mean any attempt to remove him from the werenation will have to be handled by werewolves. Correct?"

His mind works faster than mine, but even as Femke answers, I'm nodding.

"Exactly." Femke sits on the edge of her desk, chewing at her lower lip, icy eyes narrowed. "I wish there was a way around it. But if we've proved Sage—as a supposed revenant—is perfectly fine, functional, healthy, that means Caine and his people are the same. That the rules about revenants have changed."

"Not entirely." Max's deep voice startles me as he speaks. Despite his massive size, I always seem to forget he's in the room. The drach have a neutral scent when still and watchful, their aroma only apparent when they are active for some reason. Considering they are so silent when motionless, only the deep and thrumming hum of their power giving them away, I suppose it's not surprising. I turn to him as he goes on. "It was only with sorcerous interference such a transformation from true revenant—a powerless human bitten by a werewolf—to completed evolution is possible." His glittering eyes settle on Sage. "You wonder what is different about you, what made you what you are and not like Caine?"

I catch my breath, waiting for Max to go on while Sage bows his head to the giant drach.

"I'd like to know," my love says.

"We all would," Syd says while Femke nods.

Max shifts his weight, a tiny frown furrowing his brow, the faint gray tone of his skin darkening a little. "We have long been curious about your kind," he says. "We drach have watched your trapped state with some empathy but have been unable to assist, restrained as we were from interfering with this plane due to Fate's instructions."

"We have so much to thank her for," Syd says with sarcasm and a grimace.

Max nods sadly. "It is my belief," he says, choosing not to comment on Fate's instructions, "the fact you were bitten by a were in full wolf form rather than a were in half shape meant an alteration of the power transfer from him to you."

Epiphany sparkles set off like fireworks in my head. "That's it!" I turn to Sage, completing the explanation that makes perfect sense to me. "Caine bit you when he was in full wolf form, in control of all of his power."

"And that negated the trigger built in by the Black Souls?" Femke's voice is eager and I realize she loves the information chase far more than anything else. I know this is going in her file.

"The revenants you found here," I say to her, "must have been infected by weres in wereshape. But Caine chose to bite Sage as a wolf." I grin at my love. "And gave him a gift he didn't know he was granting."

"Neither did Rupe, it seems," Femke says, shaking

her head with a smile. "So now we know converting humans to werewolves doesn't have to be a death sentence."

"Though," Max's deep rumble interrupts, "I advise heavily against completely abolishing that particular law." He meets my eyes, power swirling in the diamonds of his. "Perhaps initiation similar to creating new vampires would be more prudent."

With consent and full cooperation from the ruler of the pack.

I squeeze Sage's hand, all doubt now gone in a wash of relief. "That means he is different from Caine," I say. "And we can take him down."

Femke winces, shakes her head. "Maybe not," she says. "If he's turned full wolf, too, we're back where we started."

Anger burns a slow and steady fire. "You said you'd step in if things were falling apart," I say, desperate to find a way to make this work.

Femke's blue eyes are sad as she reaches out and takes my hand. "You know I can't do that, Charlotte." She squeezes my fingers in hers. "If the Council takes over rule of your people, it will be for a very long time, not just what it takes to sort out this mess. I would really rather your people worked out their own issues if possible."

She's absolutely right, and yet I suddenly feel helpless. If Caine and his people are accepted as werewolves, this has gone back to being an internal matter with only one recourse.

I'll have to challenge the Californian who sits on my grandfather's throne. Not that I'm afraid. But if he has managed to gain the support of my people—which it sounds like he has—such a challenge could be turned down by popular vote and leave me exposed and vulnerable.

"Caine is now wereking," Sage says. Numb and unable to think, I let him go on. "That means we'll be dealing with a werewolf motivated to see me dead regardless of my status."

"Except," Syd says, "if Femke backs you and you can prove he and his people are also humans bitten and turned, he will have to accept you."

There is that. "We need to take back the throne," I say. "And there's only one way to do it."

"Two," Sage says, voice soft. "We can convince the werenation—as Caine did to Oleksander—he is unfit for the throne."

I still can't believe he succeeded. "No," I say, pulling away from Femke, from all of them, my wolf chuffing her angry agreement in my head. "In order to remove Caine from the throne, he must be challenged and defeated by the one who would rule after him."

I guess if this works, I'm going to be werequeen after all.

Someone knocks on the door, startling the group of us. All but Max who turns his big head, diamond eyes catching the light and making me think of the opulent palace I'm about to storm by force. When Femke walks over to answer it, I already know who is on the other side from the feel of their magic, and their scent coming through the cracks around the door.

Isabelle and Maksym look relieved to see me, the slim, honey haired vampire waiting for the hulking werewolf who is her boyfriend to hug me before taking her turn. Maks eyes Sage, though when my love offers his hand, the wereguard takes it firmly in his own without a hint of hesitation.

The slumped-shouldered were behind them won't meet my eyes, but his desperation seems to be gone as Raoul salutes Femke.

"I was unable to free Oleksander from his prison," my father says without preamble, voice dull and tired. "But there are enough of the werenation unhappy with how things have turned to pursue an assault on the palace."

"Why," I growl at him, "if they were so against Caine taking the throne and deposing my grandfather, are they having this sudden change of heart?" Traitors, the lot of them. How am I to rule those who would stab me in the back at the least provocation? Or trust them to uphold my challenge when I make it?

I need to have more empathy for my people. They have been through so much, taught to mistrust and be suspicious, beaten down for centuries. A handful of years of freedom haven't been enough to change their way of thinking.

Still, my grandfather has been beloved by my people all along. Why would they do this to him?

My father ducks his head in shame. "Because he had no family to support him."

I'm supposed to feel my own regret, I suppose, and guilt over my defection in favor of Sage. But all I can do is simmer in anger at my father.

"When Caine speaks," Raoul says, "the werenation listens." A frown creases Syd's face, and Femke's. "Even the most staunch supporters of the Moreau family turned against my father." Tears trickle through new lines around Raoul's eyes, the deep frown grooves that pull at his mouth, aged beyond his years. "Even I doubted Oleksander when I came to hear Caine speak." He shakes his head. "Unthinkable."

"No," Syd says. "There's another word for it." She swears softly. "Coercion."

Femke nods, grim and angry. "He's using magic against them."

"You're really surprised?" Syd begins to pace, past Max who watches her back and forth with glittering eyes. "They've been so honest and forthright all along, haven't they?" Her sarcasm cuts deep. "This revelation is hardly a shocker."

Maybe not, but it feeds my own fury. "If it can be done," I say, "it can be undone."

Syd stops her pacing. "Sounds like it's only a temporary influence?" She focuses on Raoul who nods, swallowing his grief as he visibly seems to realize what they are talking about.

"They made us believe?" My father's wolf emerges as his snout elongates then goes back to human shape, a sure sign of his rising rage. "They forced us to turn against our own?"

Femke nods, sighs heavily. "I'm afraid so." Her magic sparkles around her hand as she reaches for my father. He stands there, eyes wide, staring at her like a terrified animal, as her power gently settles around him a moment before dropping away. "Just traces left," she says. "It must be a close-contact coercion."

Syd's scowl makes her look like her mother. "He can't have the power he needs to make it permanent for so many people," she says.

"Of course," Femke says. "It must be a field of some kind, localized. That way, when the werewolves are in the presence of Caine or Rupe, they don't argue."

"And," I say with a sad sigh, knowing my people very well, "even once free of it, they would not argue with their change of heart without good reason." All that ingrained obedience has led us astray yet again.

Raoul's hands fist at his sides. "I felt nothing," he says. "I blamed myself for my weakness and that of the werewolves around me. I had no idea."

"If Charlotte is right," Syd says, "which she likely is, that was probably the plan." Syd meets my eyes. "Doubt they wanted it to be public knowledge. So a field like that, something with influence but not permanent, would serve them well."

"It would make our detection outside the werenation palace all the harder," Femke says, "and keep their secret. Which it has."

Until now. I shake my head, mind churning, searching my power for such an ability. But the wolf in me growls her anger at such a thought, that we would be capable of forcing others to believe. Wolves don't need such power. "It couldn't have been Caine," I say. Sage grunts agreement, wincing. "We just aren't capable of such an act." Even he. I can't bring myself to believe his wolf could be so corrupt.

"So their sorcerer handler has to be in on the action," Syd says, with an evil gleam of glee in her eyes. "Which means I get to have a little chat with Rupe after all this time." She's more a wolf at times than I am, I think.

"We will gather our army of werewolves loyal to the true king outside the palace grounds," Raoul says, voice vibrating with passion. "I will tell them of this deception, that they have been lied to and coerced. Our people will rebel when they know they are being controlled. And we will unseat this pretender and return Oleksander to his throne."

Femke flinches, covers her ears with her hands and hums off tune. When Raoul falls silent, she shrugs. "You didn't say that out loud in front of me," she says. "If the leader of the European Council heard of plans to usurp the duly chosen king of the werenation from his throne, I would have to act to stop you." She takes a step to the door, pulls it open. "If you'll excuse me," she says, "I'll be powdering my nose in the ladies."

Syd snorts as Femke leaves. "Now that," she says, jabbing at the door, "is a Council Leader."

I nod slowly, wishing there was more Femke could do, but grateful to her for her willingness to let us act.

"How soon can we move?" I turn to my father who even still barely meets my eyes.

"I'll need a day," he says. "To do recon and make sure we have an extraction plan for your grandfather in place." His hands clench at his sides. "Your sorcerer friends are already working something out."

I remember then Ethpeal and Demetrius went with him and feel better instantly.

"I'll give you an extraction plan," Syd says. "Tell me where he is and I'll go get him right now."

I could hug her.

"Let's hold off," Maks says. "We don't want to tip off Caine what we're planning."

"He has to know we're up to something," I say. "Roman and Viveca would have reported in by now." Likely, they had their own transportation, perhaps with Rupe himself or another sorcerer he worked with. Even if they had to use more conventional means, a simple phone call would have given Caine the advanced warning he needs to prepare for us. Because he has to know I'm coming for him.

If he doesn't, he's a fool and about to find out what it's like to cross a Moreau.

Still, I nod to Maks. "One day," I say. "We attack at this time tomorrow." Probably a good idea, anyway. I need sleep, so does Sage. And food. And a shower. Time to rest and prepare my mind. I turn to Syd who nods, stepping back to Max's side as the pair begin to glow with diamond light.

"All right," she says. "We'll see you shortly." Her mind touches mine as the veil opens and she and Max turn to enter the gap. *I'll save Oleksander*, she sends. *I promise you that.*

If he's still alive when we reach him, I send, letting her feel my practical acceptance. *Thank you.*

She doesn't answer, just leaves with the big drach leader, and I let her go. Suddenly tired, I watch Maks and Isabelle leave, Raoul pausing behind them, half-turning to me as though wanting to say something. But he, too, files out, Femke slipping in after him, gesturing to Sage and me.

"I have quarters for you both," she says. "If you'll follow Daniel, he'll show you the way." A slim page with too-long brown hair and an impish grin bounces on his toes outside the door. Sage goes with him, but Femke holds me back when I try to follow.

She stares into my eyes for a long moment before sighing heavily and releasing her grip on my arm.

"I told you once before, you can trust me," she says. "I feel like I've failed you, Charlotte."

I move to shake my head, to deny her words, but she stops me with a small, sad smile. "You needed me—you needed us—and we followed the rules. Left you out in the cold, on your own. You amaze me, do you know that?" I simply stare at her, speechless. I admire her and her strength so much, it's a bit of a shock to realize the feeling is mutual. "I want you to know, no matter what or how bad things look, I will never abandon you for the stupid rules ever again." Her fierceness wakes my wolf. "Witches are stubborn creatures, hidebound and frustrating. And I've struggled to lead my covens into more forward thinking. But I won't permit a friend to fall when she's in the right, even if it means stepping down from leadership."

I could never allow her to do that. But I appreciate

the sentiment and her loyalty. I kiss her cheek gently, let her feel the calm and determination of my wolf.

"Anything, anytime, for you, Femke," I say. And leave her there, tears on her cheeks, following after Sage while my heart warms and heals.

What have I done to deserve such friends?

FOURTEEN

Sage isn't in our room. I follow the scent of him down the hall and to the partially open door. A peek inside tells me what I already know. The bed is empty, the bathroom dark and quiet. The little page is long gone, as well. I pace around the room for a moment before returning to the hall and pursuing Sage, the deliciousness of him leading me to a stairwell at the end of the corridor.

He went up and I retrace his steps, emerging on the roof. It's dark again, night-time Oxford stretched out before me, the lip of the edge artfully crafted like the parapet of a castle. Sage is easy to spot, leaning against the stone ledge, looking out over the campus. I cross to him, my shoes grinding stone together under foot. He turns as I join him, arm slipping around my waist, snuggling me tight against his hip. I lean my head on his shoulder, feeling my body fully relax for the first time since this all began.

We're safe, with friends who love and trust us. And tomorrow I rescue my grandfather and restore him to his throne.

"I visited Oxford once before," Sage says. "I thought I might like to go to school here."

"You still could," I say. "I'm sure Femke would welcome you into the magic classes." Might be a good idea for both of us to get some real training, though I'm more comfortable with my power now than I've ever been.

Sage chuckles in my hair, lips grazing my forehead. "That," he says, "would be amazing."

I hug him tight, turning to curve my body against his, arms around his chest, lips pressing to his throat. "Sage," I whisper, voice choking off as I try to speak. "I never got to tell you how much I regret rejecting you in California."

His hands slide into my hair. "It's okay."

"No," I say, magic embracing him as I look up into his eyes. "It's not. We've come so far and I've learned so much about who I am. Who my people are. All because of you." I laugh, genuinely amused. "Imagine it took you and the attack to shake the last of the chains from my people." I kiss him, his nose cold on my cheek. "I knew there was a reason I loved you."

He laughs over my mouth. "You're welcome," he

says.

I jab him gently in the ribs and he bends, still laughing, ticklish spot turning him into a giggling boy.

"No matter what happens," I say, thinking of Femke and her promise to me, "I will never let you go."

He stills, stares down at me. "Charlie," he says. "You're going to be queen someday."

"And you," I tell him in my firmest tone, wolf growling her agreement, "will be at my side."

Sage shakes his head, sad smile curving his beautiful mouth, green eyes endlessly deep as the ocean. "I can't ask that of you or your people."

"Our people." He's one of us, now. Sage starts, eyes widening. "You're a werewolf, Sage America."

He bends and kisses me again, softly at first, then with bite and passion that leaves me breathless. The need to have him when I was in wolf shape rises again, and I wonder how I ever considered letting him go.

"I never want to hurt you." He hugs me, cradling me against him. "I know you've been through a lot, though you won't tell me what."

"Do you really want to know?" It's quiet up here, the wind soft on us despite the elevation, the night serene. It feels like perfect timing and sacrilege to the lovely night all at once.

Sage stills, nods against me. "I really do."

I tell him, a little, about Andre and my childhood. Of

117

his sons and their depraved father. About rape and pain and endless torture, of having my soul crushed only to rise again and refuse to break. I'm detached, clinical, feeling myself leave as the words leave me, the old protections of evasion and hiding still keeping me safe.

I barely remember what I say to him, but I don't tell him everything. It's enough that his body tenses and he struggles to contain his temper as his power flares against mine, bringing me back to the moment with a shuddering sigh.

"The next time I see Andre Dumont," he whispers into my hair, "I'm going to kill him and make his kids watch."

I hug Sage tighter, wondering at my reaction to his. I've always had to look out for myself and though I know Syd and Femke and my other friends are there for me, this is the first time I've felt as though another truly understands and has the need to punish the ones who hurt me. Not because it's the right thing to do, or will save the Universe, but because I matter.

And I rather like it.

"I may not get the chance," Sage says. "Won't that Erica person act against Andre if it comes out he's working with bad guys?"

I grunt my disagreement into his shirt. "Doubt it," I say. "I can't imagine Erica doing anything to rock the boat, or put herself in a position to look bad." Probably part of the reason she's so pissed off Sage and I had the run of her territory for so long.

"I always hated politics," Sage says. "I guess I better get used to them, huh?"

"I guess," I say. "Since you're going to be part of the werenation royal family."

He chuckles. "I love the sound of that."

I look up at him, my whole world his smile, his eyes, allow him feel how I feel for him.

Sage groans softly and bends over me, lips pressing tightly, tongue exploring my mouth with a demanding heat I answer. I leap, wrapping my legs around his hips, feeling him turn, pressing me against the ledge. He is hard and wanting, my body responding to the pulse of his heartbeat between us. I pant as I try to pull him closer, always closer.

Sage stiffens as I slip my hand under his shirt, down the front of his jeans. I pull away, boiling inside, needing him so much, only to watch his face slacken, his eyes roll up into the back of his head. He collapses to the ground. I grasp at him, terror replacing my burning desire, hand brushing over a cold metal cylinder embedded in the back of his neck.

I look up, too late, as a second dart whistles out of the darkness and buries itself in my throat. The anesthesia acts quickly, a trickle of magic in it subtle, but activating the drug instantly. I know not even the Enforcers patrolling the campus will feel it.

My wolf pants as I fight to stay awake, pulling in my power even as I fumble and fall on my side. I can't focus enough to counter the effects, can only lie there and watch as Kristophe and Jean Marc slink out of the dark on the other side of the roof. The elder holds a rifle in his hands, dark smile so familiar I manage a reflex twitch before the black comes to swallow me.

"Father is very disappointed in you," Kristophe's whisper in my ear is the last thing I hear, cut apart by the wail of the little girl I was as I am lost in the dark.

I wake, kicking and screaming, knowing something is wrong. It takes a long moment for me to remember what. A boot impacts the side of my head, sending me sprawling, stars bursting to life behind my eyes. I groan, roll over, tasting blood, reaching for my power as the floor beneath me leaps and I'm airborne a heartbeat.

I'm in a van, the back, hands tied behind me, feet, too. I make out the well-known scents of the Dumont brothers, the nasty stench of gasoline, sweat and dirt. The van hits another bump at speed and I'm tossed into the air before coming down hard. It's hard not to groan, winning me another kick, this time in my stomach.

I have to fight them. My magic will be more than enough to free me. And when I'm loose, I will punish them both for thinking they can hurt me, control me.

The moment I try to touch my wolf, I feel it, and despair like I've never known devours my soul.

Sorcery. Blocking me. Owning me.

My wolf howls her grief in my head as the truth sinks in and tears pool in the corners of my eyes to spill, without care, down my cheek and into my hair.

Jean Marc leans over me, teeth flashing as he grins.

"Just like old times," he says.

FIFTEEN

A hand reaches through the dark and pushes Jean Marc back. I turn to see Rupe hovering over me, scowling at the older of the Dumont brothers.

"She's not yours yet," he snaps. "Remember who your real master is, boy."

Jean Marc's scowl offers a fraction of satisfaction, enough I'm able to pull myself together. I feel Sage with me, can smell him now I'm not panicking anymore. At least we're still together. I glare at Rupe who looks down at me with a false smile. There was a time he was friends with Syd, when the two of them trusted each other. But when the Brotherhood turned him, exposed his sorcery, he turned on Syd and everything she stands for.

"Now," he says, "you've led me on quite a chase, Charlotte. You and your little friend, here." I hear Sage groan and know he's coming to. We have to find a way to communicate so we can escape. It's dark out, so I worry Femke isn't even aware we're gone and won't be until late tomorrow morning. It would be like her to let us sleep in. So we're on our own and without the means to communicate mentally.

I never thought I'd miss the ability to get into someone else's mind.

"We know what you're doing," I say, trying to keep my voice level and calm. "Why you want him."

"Oh, really?" Rupe's grin is feral. "Do fill me in."

"Just kill her." Andre's voice comes from the driver's seat. I catch a glimpse of him past Rupe, a streetlight casting illumination over the side of his face. It's in ruins still, slick and weeping, the slashing cuts I gave him reinforced with magic to ensure they never healed properly. I bare my own teeth and snap them together at the Dumont coven leader.

"Don't be silly," Rupe says, as though Andre's a complete idiot. "We need her as a bargaining chip. Just in case something happens with Caine and the others." He pats my cheek. "I want to make sure I have a replacement if he tries to cross me. And who better than the beloved wereprincess Sharlotta Moreau?"

I kick out at him but he's faster, turning to look down at something behind me. I can only guess it's Sage. "I think I have you to thank for my latest experiment's success," Rupe says. "All the others were dismal failures. But for some reason, this one worked out perfectly."

He doesn't know why Sage is different and I want it to stay that way. If Rupe touches my love, controlled or not, I'll tear him apart.

"Maybe that was the problem," Rupe says, stroking his chin like a bad super villain in a Hollywood B movie. "The samples I made had no support, no one to emulate."

Let him stay in the dark long enough to defeat him. "The revenants," I snarl, "the innocent people you infected, suffered and died because you're a failure."

He lashes out at me, almost casually, with sorcery. It's his power controlling me and I suddenly can't breathe, the blackness pressing down on my chest, forcing air from my lungs, crushing my ribcage. Darkness closes in while I gasp for air, trying even with tied hands to claw at my throat and chest, knowing this is the end if he miscalculates even a hair's breadth.

When he finally releases me, I gag on the rush of oxygen, gulping it like icy water down my parched throat.

"Regardless," Rupe goes on as though he didn't almost kill me, "I must study this latest attempt and uncover the means to recreate him." He grins at me. "Since you know all this already," he says, "do tell, what is my purpose?"

"A werearmy," I say, and from his knee-jerk reaction

of anger, I know I've hit the truth after all.

"How could you possibly—" Rupe cuts off, anger fading as he laughs. "Good guess," he says. "But correct. The controls the Black Soul sect had over you were far too easy to break." His sorcery pushes down on me again and I struggle not to panic. "Mine won't be quite so fragile. They grew weak and arrogant in their possession. I will never make that mistake. Werewolves are dangerous animals, after all." His eyes glitter with an eager need, probably to hurt me further, to prod me into giving him a reason.

I shrug as best I can despite my bonds, focusing on staying present and calm. "We figured once Belaisle gave you the boot for being a useless nit, you had to try something. And emulating your master's success had to be at the top of your list." I'm feeling reckless, though baiting him could mean my death. But I'm reasonably certain his need to keep me alive is stronger than his temper, and I've been tortured before.

Rupe doesn't strike out at me this time, though his narrowed eyes and the way he gnaws on his fingernails answers all of the questions I've had all along. Tallah and her agile mind managed to uncover the truth of the matter. Though I regret Belaisle is still alive and Rupe didn't kill him for his position after all, at least I now have confirmation of the split in the remains of the Brotherhood ranks.

Rupe's next emotionally charged statement reinforces my thoughts. "I'll show him," he snarls, though I know his words aren't aimed at me. "He thinks his are the only plans that can bring results. When he is faced with my army of super werewolves, he will fall on his knees at my feet and beg my forgiveness."

There is no question in my mind who "he" might be.

"I'm sure he will," I murmur. "That is, if I don't kill you, first."

This time it's Jean Marc who kicks me, his boot planting in my ribs and carrying me off the ground to slam against the far wall of the van. I feel Sage pressed behind me, register he's stirring, about a heartbeat before his body tenses.

And all hell breaks loose.

I feel his power surge and realize, probably around the same moment Rupe does, Sage isn't under sorcerous control. In fact, he's free, his magic massive and violent. But the power Rupe is using to keep me in his grasp still affects Sage, but in a way none of us expect.

Even through the block in my power, I sense the madness in Sage. The dark sorcery has driven him insane, even as it's fed his magic. Sage lurches to his feet, hunched over me, lashing out at the Dumont brothers while Rupe falls back with a cry. I spin, trying to reach Sage, while he throws his rage at the back doors of the van.

I can't let him go, not alone, not in this state. He's already transforming, a full wolf when he leaps out the back of the vehicle and into the darkness, his humanity crushed by the sorcerous blocks keeping his power hobbled. My caged magic batters against the restraints Rupe has place on me, fighting with everything I have to go after Sage.

Only to be jerked back away from the open doors and pulled bodily up into Rupe's enraged face.

"How is that possible?" Spittle strikes my cheeks, my lips as his red face hovers barely an inch from mine, eyes bulging in fury. "He shouldn't be able to do that." Rupe drops me, suddenly afraid, though he covers it with more anger as Kristophe groans beside him. Andre pulls over with a squeal of tires that ends in a crunch of gravel and turns to glare at Rupe.

"We have to go after him." Darkness hides the mess I've made of his face.

"Of course we don't," Rupe snaps. His eyes settle on me. "We have her."

They want to use me as bait? They'll have to kill me first. I kick out, shoving myself toward the still-open doors, not sure how I'm going to escape, but knowing I have to find Sage before they do.

A sharp pinpoint of pain and the darkness returns all over again.

This time, when I wake, I recognize the scent of straw, the feel of cold stone under my body. I'm half naked, jeans torn away, t-shirt gone, only my bra and underwear remaining. My hands are unbound, at least, feet free, but I'm groggy, disoriented, the world wavering around me as I try to focus.

"You made a mistake," Andre's voice reaches me and I whimper despite myself. He ignores me, focusing on what he's saying as my eyes adjust, no longer seeing double, trying to pull together the vision of the small, stone room, the slit of bars in a high-placed single window, the heavy steel door that is the only exit. Rupe stands at my feet, glaring down at me.

"He's never been controlled," Rupe says, words sharp with anger. "That has to be the difference."

Andre's good side is to me, hiding the ruin I made of his face. "There were no old pathways for your sorcery to inhabit."

Rupe nods once, irritation obvious. He doesn't want to have to confide in Andre, I'm guessing, sees the other man as beneath him. And yet, he's chosen his bedfellows. They deserve each other.

"So he's at full power still," Rupe says. "But his mind is mine."

"If it was," Andre snaps, "he'd be here now."

Rupe turns on him, sorcery slamming Andre into the stone wall so hard I hear the older man grunt. "I'll figure it out," he says. "Copy her pathways into him." He points at me with one vibrating finger. "Something. In the meantime, keep her alive."

Andre half-turns his head toward me when Rupe releases him. "I can do alive," he says. "As long as that's all that matters?"

Rupe shrugs, turning his back on me. "Don't disappoint me, Andre."

The Dumont leader snarls at the door as Rupe slams it shut behind him. He stares down at me, a thin strand of light coming in through the slots of the window lighting the sliced ribbons of skin on his face. He crosses past my feet as he speaks, heading for a small table propped up in the far corner.

"He's a fool," Andre says, the sound of clanking raising goosebumps on my skin. I know that sound, the flap of leather, the whisper of steel being drawn from a pouch. His implements. He's brought them with him. I know them all intimately, the edges and points and dull surfaces meant to crush and maim. "Underestimated his own cleverness and left himself open to failure." Andre turns to me, a shining spike in one hand, a curved blade in the other. I've been cut and stabbed and probed with both. The memory of the pain is almost more than I can stand and I have to dig deep inside me to find the courage to hold still and not show him fear. "Typical sorcerer arrogance. I won't make his mistake." He prods me with one shoe, still dressed in a suit, shining toe the finest leather brought to a high sheen. Andre crouches beside me, setting the tools down in the straw before shucking off his jacket and setting it aside, rolling up his sleeves while his pale blue eyes never leave mine. I shiver at the sight of his face, the four deep grooves crusted with old pus and raw from infection. "Try to fight me, Charlotte," Andre whispers, the scent of sandalwood and vanilla making the girl inside me weep. "Please, just try."

SIXTEEN

There is a method to torture, the drawing out and elongation of time and agony, maximizing the amount of pain for a subject and the equal amount of pleasure for the torturer. Andre is, and always has been, a master. Even when I was a girl and he was much younger, he had a particular knack for inflicting torment. I was only a child, but he knew exactly how far he could push me and my tiny body, how much the wolf could heal, though he would test those limits over and over again.

It had been years since Andre had me in his grasp, years since I felt the misery of his attentions. And he'd grown even more skilled. The blades slid with feather precision under my skin, the sharp barbs between my toes penetrating past the knuckles and into firm muscle. Every cracked bone is strained in such a way my wolf can heal it

131

within hours, each sliced piece of flesh already sealing when he starts on the next.

"Werewolves," he pants, his sick passion rising to flavor his natural scent with harsher tones of musk as he embeds a silver spike slowly through the soft skin between my shoulder and my collarbone, "are the perfect toys. And you, my dear," he bends to lick the side of my face as I fight the need to scream my agony into the dark room, "are the finest I've ever played with." He breathes on me, body vibrating with need. I know what comes next as he embeds the spike into the ground beneath me, pinning me to the floor. His hands fumble almost clumsily with the knife as he cuts open my bra, exposing me to him. Icy eyes travel down to my waist as he jerks free the shredded fabric of my underwear. I can't let him see my fear, my pain. I must endure this as I always have.

A tiny whimper escapes me, though I fight it. It only seems to fuel Andre's lust, as fear always has. His hands undo his belt, his button, the zipper on his pants as I sink into a place where I can be dispassionate and not care about what his body is about to do to mine. I stare up at his hideous face, once handsome, and focus all of my attention on not breaking. On staying Charlotte, intact, unreachable. He can do what he wants to my flesh, but my heart and soul belong to me.

I used to close my eyes, turn my head, try to go somewhere else when he raped me. I truly believe doing so saved me, kept me sane and unbroken. But this time, I refuse even that refuge, staring him down, pinned by his tools with my blood running from my body into the straw beneath me. I will not allow him his pleasure without a window into how much I despise and reject him.

His face flinches, anger rising as he settles between my legs. What was once hard softens almost immediately, unable to do its job in the face of my defiance. Andre grunts as he thrusts at me, but we both know it's too late. He's done, gone limp and I laugh in his face as his scowl turns to fear.

The laugh is a mistake, maybe, but I can't help it. He lashes at me, but I lunge forward against the power he uses to hold me still, pulling at the spike in my shoulder. He's distracted enough it works, and I'm free. Blood gushes from the wound as my teeth sink into the flesh of his healthy cheek and bite deep. Andre screams, shoving me back and I taste coppery heat when I let him go. He clutches at the fresh damage, staggering to his feet with his pants around his ankles, blood rushing between his fingers.

I laugh again, at how ridiculous his tiny little package looks dangling between his legs, so useless. "What's the matter, Andre?" My voice cracks and warbles, harsh in my ears. "Little girls the only ones who do it for you?"

He tries to kick me, but trips over his dropped pants and stumbles sideways, magic controls weaker than ever.

I lie back, drained from blood loss, body freed to move. I jerk loose the spike of steel and throw it at him. It clatters in the straw, lost in the dark corner, while his magic pins me down and tightens around my throat.

If I die here, I die. I can't trust him not to kill me, despite Rupe's orders. My only regret is Sage and not being able to save him. That and my grandfather, who stood up for me in the end, but was no match for a sorcerer's dishonorable ambition.

As I pass out from the lack of oxygen, I hold both of their dear faces in my mind, and send them love though I know they will never receive it.

I cough, water streaming over my face, turning on my side away from the steady stream. My shoulder still aches, so it can't be long past the time I pulled free the spike. My wolf must be hard at work trying to heal me.

"I told you," Rupe is screaming at Andre, "to keep her alive!"

I look up, find Jean Marc standing over me with a pitcher of water. He pours more from a few feet up, aiming at my mouth, I can only guess. I catch a few priceless drops as he sloshes it over my naked body, making me chase it to get a drink. When I'm done, I flip over onto my back and see Andre pressing a bandage to his cheek. He's at least managed to pull his pants up, though his shirt is still untucked, the belt undone and dangling.

"The bitch bit me," Andre snarls.

"Then don't get close enough to her to let it happen again." Rupe's anger fades, his power swirling around him at his feet like a puddle of pure shadow. "If you kill her, I will kill you and your two precious children. Do you understand?"

Andre just grunts.

"We are still tracking her little playmate," Rupe says with exaggerated slowness, as though Andre is too stupid to understand otherwise. "He followed us here and hasn't left the area, but we can't catch him if she's dead."

Sage is here? I throw my mind after him, knowing the likelihood of reaching him is slim to none, not with Rupe's controls over me. But I feel my love, regardless, like a far distant memory, the faintest trace of him.

And what I feel... makes me want to weep. Sage is gone. At last they've managed to ruin him. The man I loved doesn't exist in the mind I reach. He's devolving, maybe just to an animal, to the wolf whose shape he wears. But there is a darkness in him that makes me afraid.

He's becoming a true revenant after all.

I have to help him, put a stop to this. They can do what they want with me, but I must save Sage. Desperation drives me deeper, clutching at my power like a child holding a precious toy and I push all of what I have into a plea to the dark.

SYD!

Nothing. Not a hint or a whisper of her. She's too far, or not here on this plane. Rupe turns toward me with a grimace, but it's part smile, even as his power tightens inside me.

"Clever," he says. "But you're not strong enough, Charlotte." He gestures at Andre. "I want her too weak to fight. But alive." He stresses the word one last time.

This time, when Rupe leaves and Andre turns toward me, I feel overwhelming fear surge, uncontrollable. But not for me. For Sage.

I've failed him, in the end. And there's nothing I can do about it.

SEVENTEEN

The next time I wake, I'm groggy and can't feel my legs. It takes me some time to come fully to, to allow my wolf to heal me while I fight my patience and the need to weep and scream my rage and frustration into the empty room.

Andre took his time, with Jean Marc watching from the corner. The first light of day shone through the bars before I passed out this round. The last thing I saw was a sharp blade penetrating my abdomen, driving me, finally, into the quiet of unconsciousness.

Tingling in my feet reassures me the damage he did to my spinal cord is being handled. I turn over on my side and cough blood into the straw, my body chill and shivering. My wolf can handle a lot, can heal a great deal, but the weaker I become, the harder it will be for her to save me. I rest a moment, forehead itchy from the coarse bedding, before leveraging myself painfully up into sitting position.

I hug my arms around my naked torso, strands of my black-dyed bob sticking in the crusted blood on the side of my face. I lick slowly at my parched lips, hands exploring myself to ensure nothing is still mutilated past the point of support. I have to explore my little prison and see if there is a way to escape. And there's no telling how long Andre will be gone. The sky outside is going dark again, so he's done a lot of damage, taking my wolf nearly a half a day to heal enough to wake me. Andre must be furious to take his torture that far.

I know now it's not about pleasure for him anymore, but about punishment. I've taken the joy out of it for him. My lips curl as I grin into the empty air. Good. I'm glad I hurt him, even if only a little. Once I'm out of here, I'll make sure I finish the job.

Optimism is costly as I pull myself to my feet, leaning heavily on the stone wall to keep me upright. It's quite likely I'll never escape this, never again see Sage or anyone else I love. That I'll die here after Rupe uses me to capture Sage. But I can't quit. I just don't have it in me.

I stagger forward a step, another, until I'm under the narrow window. It's far too high for me to reach in this condition. The fresh air flowing in from outside rejuvenates me somewhat, though, and I breathe in the scent of outside a moment before turning and looking back into the room.

The small table is gone, Andre's implements. He's not stupid enough to leave them behind. I make the round of the room, eventually leaning out from the wall, using one hand to steady myself. The door is thick, solid steel, the lock a deadbolt into stone and windowless. Unless I can somehow figure out how to walk through walls, I'm trapped.

I sink into a corner, heels tucked tight, arms around my knees, and reach for my wolf. I can feel her, as I used to, more peripheral, less connected. The sorcery controls muffle me in a wet blanket of darkness. She's there, but she's even quieter than she used to be when I was under the influence of the Black Souls. Rupe is right. The Czar was arrogant, trusting too much to his track record and the status quo. Syd showed him the error of such thinking. I giggle with mild hysteria at the memory of my friend coming to my rescue. Good times.

I shake my head, knowing I'm fading into delusion from weakness and dehydration. I have no idea how much blood I've lost, though my wolf is working hard to restore me. While I know it's impossible and will never work, I push into her, feeling my wereform take shape. I'm shaky when I'm only part-way shifted and have to give up, reverting to human form again. I hoped maybe I could take my full wolf body, find a way to break the hold

Rupe has over me. But the noose is too tight around my magic and I can only sag, head falling forward, forehead pressing into my knees as I sigh out my resignation.

There has to be something I can do. I can't just sit here and wait for Andre to come back. That's what I used to do, when I was young and had no choice. I was out of options then, a little girl trapped in a life I was sure I'd never escape. But my freedom has made me restless, unable to sink into the acceptance I had as a child. It saved me, helped me build walls and barriers around what mattered most, my most sensitive thoughts and hopes. But that same resignation now feels like quitting.

And I won't quit.

I feel his mind as I lift my head, determined to find some way to act. It's as distant as before, but he's aware of me this time. My Sage. I weep into my hands, soft sobs crushing my heart as the animal brain that remains to him links with mine and howls his despair and loss.

Sage. I try to pull him into focus, to dig for some part of the man I love that might be left behind, salvage in the wreck of his humanity. But he grunts at me, growls and snarls, biting at my mind like a hurt creature cornered and in pain. I soothe him with my mind, stroking his gently and feel him calm.

Sage. This time when I speak his voice in my mind, he merely grumbles. His hold on me tightens and I catch the barest glimpse of him, running through a forest in the dark. He comes to a halt and the image leaves me, but his mind clings to mine.

There might be hope here, if I can get through to him. It's a long shot, his scrambled thoughts all about hunting and the scent of the forest, but my face is in his mind and there is a fierceness to the attachment I know is the only reason he can reach me and I him. I silently thank the love we have for each other that makes even this tenuous touch possible.

Sage, listen carefully. I show him an image of Syd. He recoils and I almost lose him but I send my own image and he stops, comes back. Slowly, carefully, I superimpose her face over mine until I can feel him panting in confusion.

Find her, I send. *Sage, find Syd. Contact her. Like you're contacting me.*

He doesn't understand, that's clear from his anxious mental whining. I touch him with my magic as best I can, then show him Syd again. *Sage, find her.*

This time, a glimmer of understanding sparks. He barks. My stomach in knots, I again touch him with my magic and then show him Syd.

He's gone with a yelp, his mind abandoning mine. I have no idea as I let my head fall back against the stone if he actually understood. It's impossible to tell. I attempt to calm my breathing, head burning with an ache, which makes opening my eyes difficult. But I tried, I did my best. And if he did get it, if I did make it clear and he is now searching for Syd, I may yet find a way from this place.

It's dangerous, sending Sage for her. He's a real revenant now, or, at least, a wolf. It might be too much for Femke, make her turn against him. But I know Syd won't give up on either of us.

I hear footsteps outside the door, the grinding sound of metal on stone. When Andre shoves the portal open and steps inside, I stare up at him with a sharp-toothed smile.

"I've been waiting for you," I say.

He pins me with magic, though I've done nothing to fight against him. I can't, not with the hold Rupe has over me. I was lucky enough to be able to break and bite him. That won't be happening again. I can already feel the strength sapping from my body as Andre brings in the small table with his shining implements on it and closes the door.

But as he turns to me, to begin again, his hatred for me replacing his need to own me, I continue to smile. It might be just like old times, but I have hope.

It'll kill him to find out he'll never win.

EIGHTEEN

I'm strong, but there's only so much abuse my body can endure. I hang on to consciousness longer than normal, clinging to my thread of enjoyment at Andre's growing frustration. When he cuts me, I laugh, the pain nothing in the face of his weakness. When he stabs me, I lick my lips and push the implement deeper, embracing the experience, using it to feed my will.

Andre's slick professionalism fails him at last, reverting to brute strength and fury, beating me finally into the darkness with a heavy, rubber mallet. I force myself to smile even as the darkness claims me, knowing no matter what he does to me from this point on, I've broken him.

How delightful.

The sun is setting again when I wake this time,

crumpled in the corner with my head at an odd angle. It's immensely painful to shift out of the twisted and shattered position, to feel my bones grind together as I gasp through the agony. My breath wheezes out of my parched throat as I slump, shattered but straightened out at least, sitting against the cold wall. The chill is soothing on the burning skin of my back and I wonder why my wolf has allowed me to wake so soon.

I can feel her struggling to heal me. She never quits, as focused as I am and her determination gives me the added strength I need to take stock. As I sit there, feeling my bones knit together, I realize she had no choice but to rouse me. Had she tried to heal me in the awkward position I was in, my body would not have reformed correctly. Instead, I rest against the wall on the dirty straw, palms up, legs spread out before me, and endure the pain that comes with my wolf restoring my battered form.

I whimper as she fuses the two breaks in my collarbone, though when she pops my ribs back into position, I have to bite my lip until it bleeds to keep from screaming. Andre's rage proves to me he knows he's failed. And regardless of Rupe's orders, I know if he gets the chance, the Dumont leader will kill me the next time he comes to visit.

There can't be a next time. I have to find a way to escape. My mind goes to Sage, to Syd, and I use what precious energy my wolf needs to heal me to reach out to my love. And find nothing. He's gone, long gone, and I can't find a trace of him. As my wolf chuffs softly and goes back to work, I do my best not to fall into despair at his absence. I have no idea how long it's been, maybe a day, since I sent him away. Surely, he could have reached her by now if he was going to. I writhe as I think of him captured, hurt or even dead, but I breathe through my fear into calm. If they had him, I would know. Andre surely wouldn't be able to resist rubbing such a truth in my face in an effort to break me. And, to be honest, though nothing else has succeeded, I fear if they do capture Sage and use him against me, I will shatter at long last.

I have to believe he's safe. My hand twitches as the muscle in my bicep weaves together, the tissue torn apart in a violent blow. I feel something sharp prod my skin and look down in the last of the light, catching a faint glimpse of silver buried in the straw.

What is it? My fingers close around it, pull it free, sticky with blackened blood. A spike, about a foot and a half long, with a smooth leather shaft for a handle. And as I stare at it, I remember.

Andre stabbed me with it. And I bit him, tearing it free from my flesh as my teeth sank into his. It flew across the room. He must have forgotten it in his fury. Left me a weapon.

It's painful to move, but I don't care. I lift the spike to my chest, cradle the steel crusted in my blood to my naked breasts and weep in joy.

My tears don't last long, dehydration not allowing me many, but I'm tired of crying long before I'm done anyway. A few hiccups break the silence in my cell as my wolf labors to save me. I lift my chin, look out the window into the darkening sky and try to be patient, to let her do her job, even as I make plans for my sharp little friend tucked against me.

My mother's face appears to me, a hallucination. My free hand rises to touch her, only to pass through her smile.

Sharlotta, she whispers.

"Momma." Another tear manages an escape. "Help me."

You have everything you need, the vision says. *I gave it to you long ago.*

She did. My training, so early, was all for this moment. Though I was taken from her too young, I realize now all the things she taught me, how to be resilient, to fight, to protect myself, were in preparation for Andre and the future in store for a young weregirl.

"Momma," I say. "Thank you."

You will survive, she says. *You always do. And you will be magnificent.*

I nod slowly, thinking of Zoe Helios, the young

Oracle. She foresaw a trauma, apologized for it. Said I'd make it through. I can't help but sob softly.

Courage, my sweet child, my mother says as she slowly fades away. *My beautiful daughter. This moment of pain is almost over...*

My fingers encounter nothing as I reach for her again, only the shadows before me as the sun sets. I cover my face with my free hand and bend over, mouth open, silent sobbing shaking my entire body. I can't control it, letting out all the grief and pain and fear in empty, heaving gasps of air. I can barely breathe around my need to choke, stomach clenching though there is nothing in it to come up. My wolf surges with new strength, a wave of healing power washing over me and sending me backward, pressing me against the cold wall as I cough on my sorrow and feel the last of my body knit back together.

I know I should rise immediately, that Andre could come at any time, but I rest there for a few moments, catching my breath, wiping at my wet cheeks. I feel calm again, almost light, though I know it's from hunger and lack of water. I'm likely in danger of my system shutting down if I don't receive sustenance. Even werewolves can die of such basic lacks given enough time and damage to our bodies. I bask in the feeling of weightlessness a moment before finally pushing myself to my feet.

I'm not as wobbly as I expect, free hand against the wall, my right holding tight to the steel spike. The door is close, close enough I don't have to expend much energy to reach it. I know it won't work, but I try using my weapon to dislodge the deadbolt, the tip just thin enough to reach. After a few tries and some grunting effort, I give up. There is no keyhole on this side, and without access to the mechanism, my sharp friend is about as useless as I am.

Well, not entirely. I have options, now. I heft it, brushing the dried blood from its smooth roundness. I can make this all go away, if I choose, can turn this on myself. Thwart Andre and Rupe, take away their bait, no longer allow them to use me against Sage, or for a toy.

But that is last resort. I may be weak of body, but my determination is as powerful as ever. I might not have access to my magic, but I grew up in the same position and it didn't stop me. And I might not have anyone to help me, but then, I've always been alone.

I will not fail myself. I will hover by this door, and I will wait for whoever comes through. And I will drive this spike through their heart and take their life before taking my own, if it comes to that.

My knees buckle a little so I crouch instead of standing, hovering by the door, eyes locked on its edge. Time ticks by, but there is only the hot metal in my shaking hand, the ache of my legs from my straining muscles and the slow, steady breathing I was taught to encourage focus.

When I hear someone approaching at last, it almost shatters my calm. I stifle a hysterical, disoriented giggle behind one hand, fingers shifting on the spike in the other, bouncing on my screaming knees as the footsteps hurry toward the door.

I can't smell him through the metal, but I know it's Andre. And I can't wait to see his face when I kill him. I lick my lips. Maybe I should make it slow, painful? But I don't have time for that. My wolf shakes me a little with a growl. I must act if I'm going to have my revenge. And maybe, just maybe, even escape.

I clamp my hand over the next squeak of excited fear emerging as laughter just as the deadbolt slowly turns. My wolf growls softly in my head as the door creaks and eases open an inch, another, until it's enough and I lunge, spike extended to kill.

NINETEEN

I catch his scent at the last second. It's the only thing that saves Piers's life.

He falls back with a cry as I collapse, still clutching my spike, at his feet. I look up at him, not believing what I'm seeing, smelling. He must be another hallucination, like my mother. But when he bends over me, his blond hair brushing over my naked skin, fearful gray eyes full of worry, I know he's really here with me.

Piers sweeps off his longcoat and drapes it over me before helping me to my feet. I fall into his arms and he hugs me close, the feel of him so wonderful I can barely stand it. My body breaks into powerful shivers, making it hard to stay upright, but Piers holds me tight in his strong arms and lets me shake out the debilitating fallout of my capture.

"Charlotte." He grips my arms, pushes me back gently, still holding me up. He swallows hard, lower lip trembling, tears in his eyes before he hugs me again. "Charlotte, you're alive." He sobs once into my hair, big hands tight and flat on my back. "It took us so long to track you, I was so afraid they…"

I kiss his collarbone past the open fabric of his button up shirt and lean away, swaying but feeling stronger, smiling though I've been through so much. It's intensely wonderful to see him, almost painful, and I touch his cheek with shaking fingers as he stares down at me. "They tried their hardest," I say, "but I'm not that easy to break."

He kisses me softly on the mouth, not a romantic gesture, but a loving and kindly one. "We have to hurry," he says, suddenly nervous all over again, glancing back over his shoulder at the partially open door. "Can you walk?"

I slip my spike into one of the pockets before sliding my arms into the sleeves of his coat, buttoning the front to cover my nakedness. I have to pull tight the belt around my narrow waist to keep the bulk from getting in my way. The reassuring weight of the spike in my hand as I retrieve it is all the strength I need.

"Let's get out of here," I growl, heading for the door. The hall outside is more stone. We must still be in England somewhere, a castle, maybe? "How did you find me?"

Piers hovers at my shoulder, the two of us slinking down the stone hall toward what looks like a set of stairs at the end. A bigger window shows me an elevated view of the darkened countryside. We must be in a tower of some kind, because the stairs are curved to the right when I reach them, descending down and out of sight.

"We tracked you through Andre," Piers says. "I convinced the others he was probably behind it, not Rupe. Or, at least, not alone."

I reach out and squeeze his hand. "Smart," I say.

Piers shrugs, gray eyes worried, staying close to me. "I just wish it hadn't taken so long to find him. I'm sorry, Charlotte." He looks away. "I can't imagine what he did to you."

And he'll never know. "It's over," I say. "And Andre will pay for what he's done." I must put this behind me, focus on the reason I'm here in the first place. "Where is Syd?" I try not to let my heart sink. If it was Piers who figured out where to find me, that means Sage didn't find her after all. Which leaves the question: where is he?"

"I don't know," Piers says as we come around the final turn and reach the bottom. "She disappeared before you were taken."

I stop him, hug him hard one last time. "Thank you."

"You're welcome." He clears his throat. "We have to go."

I nod as I pull away, wiping at my nose and wet cheeks. More tears. I didn't think I had the moisture to spare. "Can't we just take one of your tunnels out?"

Piers shakes his head, arm around me as he guides me down a wider hall, decorated this time, with a heavy medieval influence. Definitely a castle of some kind. I drift past a suit of armor as he whispers.

"Rupe has this whole place blocked with sorcery," my friend says. "I can't cut through it. We have to make it outside his shielding."

"He's controlling my magic." I almost choke on those words. "Can you free me?"

I feel his power crawl over me, my wolf shuddering at his touch.

"Not until we're outside," he says, pausing at the top of another, grand set of stairs. The place feels silent to me, as though no one lives here, but the lights are on and it feels well maintained. "It should be safe, the others are creating a diversion. Let's go."

I follow him, not asking who he means, can only guess it's the usual suspects. And that guess is confirmed as a dark-haired woman hurries from a side corridor and up the stairs toward us, her blue eyes locked on me. I almost fall into Ethpeal's arms as she races to greet me and flings her arms around me, holding me so tight it's hard to breathe. Who needs breath when I have her there?

"Piers." She releases me long enough to snap orders. "Go help Demetrius and Miriam. I'll take Charlotte the rest of the way out."

He hesitates, but she smacks his arm and he nods with a grin, rubbing the offended spot.

"Yes, ma'am," he says, hurrying away, though he looks back as he reaches the bottom step, just before disappearing down the same corridor from which she appeared. Ethpeal spins me toward her, face grim and angry.

"The Steam Union is coming," she says, guiding me down at last. "And I want that boy to have lots of room to run from his mother if she decides to try to arrest him."

Poor Piers. I understand his reasoning for leaving the Steam Union. I'm not a huge fan of Eva Southway myself. But I fear he did it for me, the wrong reason to abandon his people.

"Don't you worry about him," Ethpeal says as we reach the bottom floor. I glance sideways, realizing the castle isn't empty after all. A crumpled collection of bodies lie on the marble floor, one of them with short, dark hair and another with long, the Dumont brothers unconscious.

Or dead. I can hope for dead.

"We can hope Eva will be too occupied with Rupe to worry about her son," Ethpeal says, hurrying me forward, not to the same hall Piers ran down, but the opposite way. My stomach heaves as she stops me at a cart and forces a bottle of water into my hands. "Drink as much as you can. But hurry."

I gulp the cool water, emptying the bottle in less than thirty seconds. My insides cramp, protesting the onslaught of precious liquid, but my wolf works her magic, and I'm eagerly reaching for another from Ethpeal's strong hands a moment later. I take the third with me, making short work of my second banana, craving meat but not having time to be choosy.

Ethpeal doesn't flinch when a pair of young men emerge at a run from the corridor up ahead. A giant wall of black hits them like a train engine, bowling them over. She swears softly, too quiet for me to make out the words with my heart pounding in my ears at the forced exercise, but I've heard her repertoire and can guess she's using her favorites.

"Piers says your sorcery is blocked," I say.

"From making an escape route, yes," she says. "But I can still pack a punch. In here." She shoves me through a doorway, using her shoulder to push open the heavy door before slamming it shut behind her. I follow, feeling better for the water and bit of food, to a glass door at the far end, leading out into a lush garden. The outside air is a balm on my soul, deep breaths of it filling me with the scents of roses and other flowers, dirt and clean, open sky.

Something rumbles off in the distance, on the other side of the house. Ethpeal pushes me down the stone path through the garden and into the open lawn on the other side. I look back at the squat castle, up at the tower that was my prison, even as a black sheet of flame engulfs the property. I stumble and fall on my hands and knees in the fragrant grass as Ethpeal tumbles to the ground beside me, the rolling pressure of the assault a physical blow.

"I guess Eva made it," Syd's grandmother grins at me. "As much as I admire her gumption, I'm happy to miss the crap hitting the fan." She stands, offers me her hand. I take it, hoisting myself up, only to find myself in her arms again.

"We really have to go," she whispers in my ear.

"I know," I say. "Ethpeal, thank you." Now I can cry, I have the water in me to do it.

She pushes me away, roughly swiping at her own cheeks. "Silly girl," she says. "You are family." Her eyes widen, gaze over my shoulder, power gathering even as I turn and realize we're not alone.

Andre, his resurrected sons behind him, run from the edge of the garden, looking back over their shoulders as they flee.

TWENTY

They are no match for Ethpeal's sorcery, but it's not her I'm worried about. I raise one hand to stop her as she gestures, a sheet of black flame twisting outward from her feet as the trio of Dumonts come to a skidding halt on the slick grass.

"They belong to me." I don't meet her eyes, don't need to. I can feel her power retreating, surrounding me even as Andre pales, damaged face mottled with crusted pus, eyes bulging at the sight of me. He knows he's in trouble as Ethpeal's power dives inside me and breaks the hold Rupe's magic has over my soul. I feel myself freed even as I throw my essence into the wolf, leaping at Andre's throat.

Jean Marc tries to block me with magic, a hoarse shout following a ball of witch fire he hurtles at my head.

But I snap at it as my power blazes, devouring the energy and channeling it inside me. Kristophe flees, screaming like a girl, and I let him go even as my front paws impact Andre's chest, carrying him to the ground.

I ignore Jean Marc, feeling Ethpeal's sorcery behind me, knowing she will keep him occupied, though I hope she doesn't kill him just yet. I'll track down the younger of the Dumont brothers when I have leisure. Right now, everything I want is right here, under the full weight of my wolf body, staring at me with absolute terror.

His magic is as powerful as ever, but I'm in the full throes of my perfect shape and driven by the need to hurt him. Perhaps the sorcerer who guards me offers her aid as well, but I don't notice if that's the case, or care. Blue eyes bulge at me, the infection in his face oozing out in a bubbling mix of blood and pale green jelly from the broken crust over the slices on his face. The bite on his other cheek has been uncovered, bandage gone, bright red around my teeth marks.

He smells ill, dirty, as though the very core of him as become infected. I sneeze in his face, spraying him with wolfy snot and saliva, barking a satisfied laugh at his horrified expression.

Andre. I send the thought directly into his mind. *Hello, Andre.*

He struggles under me, but I push harder with my magic, containing him.

How are you feeling? I sniff deeply. The damage I've done, the infection I scent, it's all through him now. Not the same as a werewolf's bite does to a human, but deeper, fed by my hate and magic, spreading illness throughout him. I've done him far more hurt than I originally intended and it makes me happy. He's suffering, his power reduced by the injury. While his coven sustains him, I can feel the rot inside and know it's only a matter of time before he dies in agony and madness.

I could kill him here and now, end his pathetic life. But the thought of him withering away, unable to stop the degradation happening to him, appeals to me at a most basic, child-like level. The girl I was giggles her wicked glee as I back away from him and allow myself to transform to human, standing naked over him, the coat Piers gave me discarded on the grass behind me.

"Have a nice what's left of your life, Andre," I say, waving him off. Ethpeal comes to my side, frowning, but doesn't argue when Jean Marc makes a lunge for his father and drags him to his feet. The pair stagger off into the darkness as Syd's grandmother hands me the longcoat. I slip inside it, shivering in the night, but with pleasure.

I will find Andre in his last days and sit at his bedside and watch him die slowly.

Such sweet vengeance.

As I turn to Ethpeal, I feel the sudden pressure of

sorcery, but not hers. She shakes her head at me as I cinch the belt of the coat tight and turn to find Eva Southway striding across the grass toward me. Piers's handsome mother looks pissed, her close-cropped blonde hair spiked up as though as angry as she is. I hold my ground, glaring back at her, noting Piers's presence behind her as she comes to a sudden halt only a few feet away, a small group of her people surrounding her.

"Charlotte Girard," she says, crisp and angry.

"Leader Southway." I don't bow my head and she's lucky I used the honorific considering the time I've had. She's done everything in her power—including turning against her own son—to capture Sage and I and I can't help but hold the pursuit against her.

"Where is the revenant?" She looks past me at Ethpeal, frown deepening. "I should have known you'd be here."

Demetrius pops his head around Eva's shoulder and waves at me with a sweet smile. I grin and wave back.

The Steam Union leader glares over her shoulder before sighing. "Well?"

I shrug, dull anger replacing everything. "I don't know," I say. "He's gone."

One of her fists thumps against her thigh as her tall, lean body snaps around to face Piers. "If you're hiding the fugitive—"

"Give it a rest, Mum," he says, leaving her side to

160

stand with me. Eva watches with narrowed eyes as Demetrius, with a wink and a grin, cross the grass to join me. "I don't answer to you any longer, remember?"

"You're a rogue in my territory," Eva snaps. "Is that how you want this to play out?"

Piers's anger shows at last as he shakes his head at her, long fingers jabbing the air between them. "You're missing the most important point," he says, voice bubbling with temper. "There's another rogue you've let run rampant and he's the reason we're having this damned conversation in the first place."

Eva's jaw jumps but she nods once, sharp as a knife cut. "We're tracking him," she says, a hint of petulance in her voice. I know the Steam Union has suffered in the past, small and weak in number, unable to act though the need was there. But Eva isn't doing her people any favors by holding back now. Or by playing by old rules.

I should talk. I've only learned that lesson myself. Seems we all have a ways to go.

"Where is Syd?" I was sure she would be here and it hurts she's not.

"I have no idea," Eva says, anger returning. And resentment hovers in her now. Bitterness. Well, if she's not going to act, someone has to. And Syd has never been one to stand by and let the bad guys get away.

"Maybe you should be chasing the real criminals," I say. "Instead of standing here, berating your son and treating *me* like a criminal."

"I won't let the revenant get away." Eva's voice practically vibrates with passion. And I understand, then, why she is so eager to catch Sage. I can smell it in her fear, feel it in the waves of anxiety she carries around with her.

"Your people didn't make him." I take a step toward her, hand outstretched. "He's not your responsibility. And no one blames you or the Steam Union for his creation. We know Rupe acted on his own."

She shivers, fury all over her face, but doesn't comment. I take that as a good sign and go on, feeling so sure of myself, I know this is my chance to get through to her and diffuse the situation.

"Rupe is still Brotherhood," I say. "But he's working on his own." I shrug. "At least, that's what he told me. Belaisle appears to have fallen from grace and Rupe wants to replace him. You are in a powerful position, Eva. To take down the last of the Brotherhood and ensure the dominance of the Steam Union. Sage is my responsibility." I thump my chest with one fist, hoping she listens, needing her to run off and do whatever it is she's going to do and leave me to finish this fight. "Rupe and his sorcerers are yours. I'll let you do your job, if you leave me to mine."

She doesn't move a long moment, or react, though I feel her anger ebbing, her fear retreating. When she finally nods and turns from me, her mind reaches for mine.

Keep my son safe, she sends. *Or I'll hold you personally responsible.*

She and her people vanish through a black tunnel, leaving the rest of us behind on the cool grass. I watch her go, heart tight, chest so compressed by the need to hold myself back, it's hard to breathe. The moment the doorway slips shut, I turn to my friends who stare at me with expectation.

"Let her try to find Rupe," I say. "I already know where he went."

"To the palace," Piers says, a tiny smile twitching the corner of his mouth. "Mum's going to be pissed, Charlotte."

"Let her be," I say. "This is my fight and no one is going to keep me from winning it."

TWENTY-ONE

The words are barely out of my mouth when the air over head explodes with blue fire. I look up as Femke and her Enforcers appear, holding my place as she plunges to the ground and runs to me headlong. Another enthusiastic embrace, another moment of tears as she hugs me tight, rocking me back and forth as she chokes her own sobs into my ear.

When we pull apart, she turns me slowly around, examining me, though all my physical hurts are now healed. Her sorrowful eyes tell me she's aware I didn't escape this entirely unscathed, but I shake my head at her, scattering the tears from my cheeks as I deny the questions she wants to ask.

"Andre was here," she says. "I have Enforcers

rounding him up. He'll stand trial and be executed, if he harmed you in any way."

I take her hand, pull her to me. "Let him go," I whisper. "Send him home and ban him from your territory if you feel the need, but don't harm him."

She stares into my eyes. "Charlotte—"

"Please." I wink at her, letting her see and feel my wolf. "He has a horrible end coming to him, Femke. I want him to enjoy every minute." I then share with her the last touch of him I felt, the infection, the rot, and she shudders before nodding.

"As you wish," she says, eyes bright with more tears.

Cursing, stumbling, the Dumont brothers and their father are herded from the dark by a pair of Enforcers. The moment they spot Femke, the three of them begin their protests, but the European Leader merely holds up her hand and they fall silent.

"You are culpable," she says in an icy voice matching her Scandinavian beauty, "in the kidnapping of a free werewolf, communion and cooperation with a rouge sorcerer, and invading my territory without permission when you were asked to leave Europe."

Andre's lip curls, pulling against the wounds on his face. He has some arrogance left to him, it seems, though he refuses to look at me and his hands shake when he points at Femke.

"We had nothing to do with any of it," he lies, bold as

you please. "We were coerced."

A typical and expected excuse. Femke's anger doesn't leave her, but she shrugs and gestures to the Enforcers guarding the Dumonts.

"I couldn't care less," she says. "You're not mine to deal with any longer. Your own Council Leader will have to ponder your fate. But hear me, Andre Dumont." Blue fire crackles around her, an ice queen, as stunning as she is deadly. "If you set one foot in my territory ever again, I will have you killed on sight, without prejudice, and anyone who succeeds in ending your life will be rewarded by me personally."

Andre twitches, old hate and anger simmering in his eyes. He turns from her with a sharp bark at his sons who slink off after their father. I wish Syd could see it. Their utter defeat almost makes everything worth it.

No, not quite. That will take much more than simple defeat.

Blue fire flares and the Dumonts are gone, back to America. I'll pay Andre a visit when the time comes. For now, I have to find Sage. And rescue my grandfather. The timing is finally right. The trauma is over and Zoe was right—I survived it. Came out stronger on the other end, just like I always do.

I turn to Femke and hold out my hand. "Is the army still waiting?"

She nods. "And have been for days. Since you were

taken." Her face crumples, the stormy chill of her leader persona fading as the woman who cares about me returns. "Charlotte," her voice is suddenly thick and heavy with regret, "I'm so sorry, this is my fault."

"No," I say. "It's Rupe and Andre's. But the latter will wait." I rub my arms through the fabric of Piers's coat. "Where is Sage?"

The Council Leader's sadness is my answer. "We don't know," she says. "When we tracked Andre here, we assumed Sage would be with you."

I reach out for my love, but can't find a trace of him. The thrill of panic that follows I smother with focus. "And Oleksander?" I hold myself rigid against my fear of the inevitable. "Is my grandfather still alive?" I almost don't want to ask.

Femke looks suddenly relieved as Ethpeal steps up and slips her arm around my shoulders.

"Safe, for now," she says. "Demetrius and I are just waiting for the order to go in and get him."

I nod. "If I'm right and Rupe is with the werewolves, he could be blocking your ability to travel there, too."

She shrugs. "Then we'll kick his ass until he begs us to stop."

I grin at her. Hayles. I love them all.

I'm clean. It feels amazing and though I probably didn't have time to shower, I couldn't bear the feeling of myself any longer. I'll take time for a more lengthy bathing after this is done, but for now, the five minutes of super-hot water and harsh scrub gloves with heavy-duty soap have made me feel alive again.

I devour a plate of steak and mashed potatoes, slathering on a healthy helping of gravy while my friends talk around me. My wolf chuffs her pleasure as the rare meat grinds between my teeth. I almost groan in pleasure at the first bite, barely taking time to breathe as I dig into the first meal I've eaten in days.

Three days, as it turns out. I refuse to think back, not yet. There might be time later to allow myself to curl into a ball and relive the moments of pain and horror with Andre. Maybe with Sage by my side to hold me and stroke my hair, whisper his love for me. But not now, not until he is restored, my people are safe, and my grandfather is free.

Isabelle and Maks sit across from me, the delicate vampire smiling softly, sadly, while Maks tries to steal a bite of my steak. I stab at him with my fork, growling as I hunch over my plate, and he grins at me as if it's funny.

It kind of is.

"Caine and his pack aren't sitting comfortably in the palace," Maks says while I finish my dinner. "The coercion is wearing thin without the sorcerers to reinforce it."

"Would Rupe have abandoned Caine to his fate?"

Femke taps her fingernails against the side of her glass. "The Californians are Belaisle's creations, are they not?"

I nod, swallow so I can speak. "He confirmed it," I say. "He wants Sage. And I wouldn't put it past him to drop Caine like a hot rock if he could have something more valuable in exchange."

"But you still think Rupe is at the palace?" She doesn't doubt me, I can tell that, but she has to ask.

I think about it, chewing more slowly before shrugging. "It's the only thing I can think of," I say. "We can check when we free Oleksander. And if he's not there, then we go to California." I know Femke has already alerted Tallah Hensley and her coven. I overheard her as I entered after my shower. So if Rupe does show up back on the west coast of America, we should have some warning.

"Sounds like a plan." Femke nods, blonde hair swinging around her pale cheeks. "The werearmy is prepared to move?"

I don't look at him as my father speaks. He won't meet my eyes, either, so I give up trying. "We are," he says, sounding more like himself than he has for years. More like he did when my mother was alive. Hopefully, his shift in attitude will last. I need him to lead the werewolves against Caine so I can sneak in and surprise him.

I set down my fork, finally full, as Isabelle speaks up.

"The vampire families are both willing to offer assistance to the werenation." She dimples at me. "My queen wanted me to assure you she's one hundred percent in favor of returning the Moreau family to the throne and will act on your orders."

That's a huge offer. Centuries of animosity between vampires and werewolves technically ended when Syd freed us. The Black Soul's sorcery had been the source of our mutual hatred, it turned out, but old habits die as hard as old wolves. There are still those among my people who hold unwarranted hatred for vampires, and vice-versa, I'm certain.

I nod to Isabelle, mentally sending love to Sunny for her generosity. It's hard to accept, though. The pride of the werenation, hovers inside me yet. But I square my shoulders and embrace this new sense of partnership, knowing the more bodies I have for a frontal assault, the easier it will be for me to come in the back door.

"Please offer my thanks to Her Majesty and my acceptance of her offer as the heir of the werenation." I'm not, officially. Caine has seen to that. But no one here seems to think it's anything more than semantics.

I turn to Femke, knowing what she'll have to tell me in answer, but wanting to ask anyway. Since offers are being made, and all.

"Council Leader Svennson," I say, holding my trust for her in my heart as her blue eyes, unreadable, lock on mine. "I would ask for the help of the European Witch Council in official capacity as the heir to the throne of the werenation. My people need your help and I would request you intercede on our behalf."

Femke holds my eyes a long moment. "Thank you for your belief in us," she says. "Such a request is a huge step for the werewolf race, and an even bigger one for all the magic nations. It harkens a new dawn of cooperation and trust in each other."

I sit, tense and wary, but hopeful as she pushes her glass away.

"Though it might require a meeting of the Council, I'm making an executive decision." She stands and the rest of us join her as she circles the table and comes to my side. "The European Witches Council recognize you, Sharlotta Moreau, as the true heir to the throne of the werenation and declare Cicero Caine a usurper." I bite my lips to keep from shouting my excitement, heart pounding as she goes on. "Because of the state of your nation, I and my people choose to support your efforts to reclaim your throne and liberate your race from said usurper."

I reach for her hand, grasp it tight, as Femke's mind touches mine.

You and Syd, she sends with a thrill of her own nervous excitement, *are a terrible influence. And I love it.*

You could be deposed from your leadership for this, I send.

They'll never do it, she sends, smiling. *I scare the crap out of them. Besides, I'm tired of politics. If this is the end of my career, so be it. I'm sure there's a certain coven in North America that will take me in if I'm outcast.*

I hug her. *And a grateful werenation that will do the same.*

Femke kisses my cheek and turns to the others. "A coalition of magical races." She grins. "I'm speechless."

TWENTY-TWO

I sit on a velvet-cushioned bench behind the throne at Castle Wilhelm, hands folded in my lap though I long to wring them out of my need to act. Sunny sits across from me, handsome Frank Hayle standing behind her, sympathy in his blue eyes as he smiles at me. Isabelle sits next to her queen, tense, but eager as the ruler of the Wilhelm clan turns to her tall, attractive counterpart lounging next to me beneath the stained glass window. Sebastian's dark curls shine in the light as he nods to Sunny.

"Clan DeWinter is at your service," he says to the queen before smiling at me with his charismatic flair turned on to maximum. "And at yours, Your Highness."

Everyone is calling me that, ever since Femke's little speech. I know it's a reinforcement of assurance. They need to feel they are doing the right thing, and the constant reminder is their way of shoring up their own courage. Though, in Sebastian's case, I know he's doing it to tease me because he can.

I don't argue with the title. I have to at least try to play the part if this is all going to be even quasi-legal. Femke is right now assembling the Council to tell them of her decision and I can only hope they don't kick her out of Oxford.

I will not worry about her. Femke is more than capable. And regardless of whether or not I have her assistance, I'm taking back the palace and saving my grandfather.

"Has anyone seen Syd?" I am concerned for her, if only because no one has brought her up and she hasn't made an appearance.

Frank shrugs, a little frown replacing his smile. "Mir told me Max dragged her off before we found out you were taken. Something about an emergency in the veil." His sympathetic expression makes me almost angry, but not at him, or at Syd. At the fact he thinks I would be angry or upset at her for not being here. "She has no idea you were taken, or she would have been here for you." I wave off his assurance, since I already know it's true. But that also means Sage went looking for someone who wasn't here on this plane. So where did he end up? "I'm sure she'll be back as soon as she can."

"Her tasks with the drach take priority," I say, only a tiny petulant part of me wishing it wasn't the case. "And the hunt for Sage?" I haven't been able to track him, even with full power at my command. Which leads me to two fears—either he's dead and lost to me, which I refuse to accept, or he's shielded.

And only one kind of power would be able to keep him from me.

Blue fire shimmers and Femke steps through. She looks harried, points of red at the tips of her cheekbones standing out against her pale skin, but she nods and smiles at me, if with a crackle of anger in her.

"The Council agrees with my decision," she says, crisp, sharp and I know she's paid a price for the win. "We will assist. But, this must happen by the book."

"Which means?" Sunny greets her with a bow of her head, gesturing for Femke to sit. She does, pulling off leather gloves, her black robe shoved back from her button up and black dress pants.

"We have to give them a chance to surrender," Femke says. "At least, my Enforcers do."

"Leaving the rest of us to hit first and ask questions later," Sunny says.

Femke winces. "Not exactly." Her deep sigh stirs my empathy and I pat her hand as she goes on. "They've agreed to the coalition," she says. "But only if I'm running it. Which means the forces must be at my command and follow my rules of engagement."

This is a problem. Sunny appears instantly irritated, though Sebastian laughs, shattering the tension before it has a chance to build too far.

"How typically witchy," he says, winking at Femke. "The DeWinter Clan is willing."

Sunny stares at him with open shock. "You can't be serious."

He shrugs. "If something were to happen in this first coalition, a few of our people acting without our knowledge or permission, why, that would simply have to be blamed on the infancy of our agreement, would it not?"

Sunny's anger fades into a gorgeous smile. "I suppose that's true," she says before nodding to Femke. My witch friend looks slightly ill, but when she laughs with them, I know she'll be fine.

"I don't want to know," she says. "Okay? Just don't tell me and it will all work out."

I scent him before he appears, though this time I look up and greet my father with a nod when he joins us. "News," he says abruptly, collapsing onto the bench beside Femke.

"Tell us." She turns to him, offers her hand glowing with power. He rejects her generosity, head hanging, weariness rolling from him, tainting his scent.

"The sorcerer Rupe is indeed at the palace," he says.

"I've only just come from there and have seen him with my own eyes."

Sunny raises her fingers to a pair of young vampires who hover nearby, both dressed in cloaks, looking back and forth between their queen and my father. They nod to her and retreat and I realize they must have volunteered to be his transportation.

"Perfect." Piers rubs his hands together. He's on a low bench a few feet from me, long legs stretched out before him. "That leaves me free to act and Mum can't say a word about it."

"She'll expect you to include her," Femke says. Sighs. "And the Council will, too."

"The Steam Union aren't an official part of this coalition," I say.

She rolls her eyes at me, but she's smiling. "You're getting good at this, you know."

I fake shudder. "Save me."

"There is more." Raoul leans around Femke and finally meets my eyes. "They are planning to kill Oleksander at dawn. They know you're coming for him and I'm certain this knowledge came to me as part of a trap to capture you."

"Maybe so," I say, "but are they aware we're all working together?"

He shakes his head. "I do not know," he says. "I doubt it."

"A werewoman and her friends aren't much of an army," I say. "Even with such powerful people on my side. But a gathering of magical forces such as has never been seen before?" I find myself grinning in wonder. "Let's see if their little plan can be turned on them."

Raoul is quiet as the others murmur their assent. "Oleksander," he says, "isn't the only bait for this trap, Sharlotta."

And in that moment, my fear is realized. "They have Sage."

He nods, misery rising from him. Why is he so upset? Surely not for me. He's always been too selfish to care about the hearts of others.

"The wolf he's become," Raoul says, "is a revenant."

I shake my head. "That's the sorcerer control," I say, though I have no idea if I'm right, if Sage will return to me after Rupe's hold over him is broken. "Shutting down his mind. Once he's free, he'll be fine."

Even Femke hesitates, but I cut off all argument by standing, jaw set and determined. "Sage is mine to deal with, no matter his condition. Agreed?"

No one moves.

"I will go in alone," I say, voice quiet, deadly. "I will rescind my request for aid and ban all of you from the werenation and this conflict. Sage is mine."

"Like hell you will." And Syd is there, arms crossed over her chest, pony tail swinging as the cut in the veil she traveled through seals shut behind her. I beam a smile at her, a tremor taking me at the sight of her. There were moments, in Andre's care, I wondered if I'd ever see her again. Having her here, so close to me, her familiar presence and scent giving me courage, I can't imagine we'll fail.

The gathering of leaders all nod at last, even Femke, though she is the final one to do so, blue eyes on Syd.

I exhale heavily and shake out my tense hands. "Excellent," I say. "Shall we invade my nation?

TWENTY-THREE

Our war meeting finished, the others leave Syd and I alone for a moment, though by design or accident, I'm uncertain. My limbs tremble as she closes the distance between us, her face crumpling into hurt before she hugs me in fierce need.

Someone informed her of my captivity, that much is obvious. She doesn't whisper an apology or blame herself, but I know both run through her to the bottom of her soul. The Dumonts are witches, after all. But I can't allow her to shoulder a burden that's not hers.

"I'm here," I say softly in her ear, only for her hearing though the others have retreated far enough, backs to us, I know they can't discern my words. "And I'm safe." My arms tighten reflexively around her as she nods against my shoulder. "As for the rest, it will resolve itself someday, when the ones who hurt me have suffered sufficiently."

Syd leans back, wipes at tears on her cheeks with the shoulder of her t shirt, blue eyes sad. "Can I watch?"

I laugh, without pain or sorrow behind it, just for the joy of being with her. Our bond might be gone, but I will always feel better when I'm at her side.

"It will be messy," I say, "and involve screaming."

She shrugs, hands diving into her pockets. "Earplugs are cheap," she says. "And I'll stand back."

We grin at each other, a pair of crazy women, but I know her offer is real and I love her for it.

"I understand if you have to go again," I say. "The safety of the veil comes first."

She shakes her head, brow furrowed. "Not this time," she says. "Max and his crew can handle the mop up. I would never have gone if I'd known you'd been kidnapped." There's her guilt again, shining in her face. Her hands twitch in her pockets. "I should have stayed and made sure you were safe. But Femke assured me she'd keep you from attacking until I got back." Her blue eyes fill with tears. "I didn't meant to be gone so long, but time in there," she jerks her thumb over her shoulder, referring to the veil, "goes by so differently than out here."

I touch her cheek with my fingertips, brushing back a strand of her hair won free from her ponytail. "You did exactly as you needed," I say, "and all is well."

Her lips twist in protest, but she sighs and nods. "What happened?"

"Do you really want to know?" I won't tell her, regardless. She carries enough with her already and I am strong enough to endure.

Grim, she reaches for me, fingers tight on my wrist. "I really do."

I manage a smile, tight and angry, but not at her. "It doesn't matter now," I say. "Femke has ensured the Dumonts will never set foot in Europe again. And though I hold out little hope for her support, perhaps Erica will deal harshly with them for their involvement in this mess."

Syd's eye roll and wry snort mirror my own feelings. "Likely," she says. "The day Erica actually does something useful is the day the Universe comes to an end." She winces at her reference, makes a little sign with one hand in rainbow light. "Knock on elements." Her eyes tighten, a few tiny lines showing, the crease between her brows so much like her mother's I almost smell lilacs. "You're more patient than I am. I'd have just killed them and been done with it."

We both know she's lying. Syd avoids such ends at all costs, even more now she'd been the deliverer of Ameline Benoit's death. The girl deserved it, and I am still proud of Syd for doing what she had to, to protect her family and the Universe. But she is mostly bluster and temper, though I'm not complaining.

"Forgive the intrusion." We both turn at the sound of Piers's voice, though I felt his approach moments before he spoke. "I'm about to contact my mother and was wondering if the two of you would like in on the conversation?"

Syd links arms with me. "Wouldn't miss it," she says.

I hesitate to speak, though we follow Piers to where Sunny and Frank await with the rest of our friends. Only then do I notice Alison, Sebastian's shadow and Syd's former best friend turned ghost turned who knew what, hovering on the periphery. She still held herself apart from the rest of us, despite all the years that have passed. I gesture for her to join us and see the surprise in her eyes, the gratitude, before she slips ahead and stands at Sebastian's side.

"Why have we decided to include the Steam Union?" The last we talked, I assumed we were leaving them out of it.

Piers shrugs. "Even with such powerhouses as Ethpeal and Demetrius," he bows to them while they grin back, "there are only three of us. We have no idea how many friends Rupe has brought with him."

"If any," I say.

My father shakes his head. "There are a number of sorcerers at the palace," he says. "Young and inexperienced from what I can tell, but they follow Rupe's orders."

Syd releases me, turns to face me. "It's up to you," she says. "I can back up Piers if you want to keep Eva in the dark."

They wait for me to answer while I turn it over in my mind. When I finally nod to Piers, he looks relieved.

"Very well," I say. "But she must agree to the same terms as the rest of us." I gesture at Femke. "If she won't accept the leadership of the Council, she's not invited."

"Agreed," Femke says, face stormy. I know she won't take "no" for an answer.

Piers's black power pools at his feet and, within a moment, a gaping tunnel of darkness opens behind him. I hold myself still as Eva and a string of her sorcerers enter the throne room at Wilhelm. She looks angry, frustrated, but not aimed outward, so I can only hope she agrees to our terms.

"Eva." Femke steps forward, face cold. "You're late to the party."

"Maybe if I knew there was one," Piers's mother answers, equally as chill. "My invitation seems to have been waylaid." She meets my eyes a moment, drifts her gaze past me as though I'm unimportant, settles on Syd. My jaw jumps in anger. Considering I'd shown her a measure of kindness not so long ago, her attitude rubs me the wrong way.

"Oh, do get over yourself, Mother." Piers's taunt tightens the skin around his mother's eyes. "You're here now, aren't you?"

"We have confirmation the rogue sorcerer Rupe and some of his companions are right now in residence at the werewolf palace in Ukraine." Femke holds up one hand as Eva tries to speak. "The Council has agreed to a coalition force to approach the usurper wereking and demand the surrender of the sorcerers and the Californian pack we believe were created and not born." Eva doesn't try to interrupt this time, just listens. "My Enforcers, along with a force of Wilhelm and DeWinter vampires," both rulers nod their agreement, "choose to stand with the true heir to the throne." Femke's cloak rustles at her feet as she straightens her shoulders. "We would have the Steam Union join our coalition and stand with us."

Eva's frown eases slightly, though she still smells cautious. "Under your command, I assume?"

Femke nods. "That is the requirement of the Council," she says. "We do not wish to tread on the toes of autonomous magic races, but it has long been known by all if we are forced to do so, we will not hesitate." Considering how many more witches there were than the rest of us combined, I knew Femke had the power to follow through if she had to. Mind you, she and her Enforcers would be no match for the Steam Union, no matter their small numbers, sorcery able to counter any magic. And yet, I wouldn't put it past Femke to have developed her own sorcerers to counter such a threat.

Eva shrugs at last, resistance gone, though I can sense a taut anger in her still as she replies. "Very well," she says. "The Steam Union welcomes the opportunity to work with other races to our mutual benefit."

Femke nods, turns in a crisp half circle outward. A tall, handsome witch in a black robe bows to her.

"Albert," she says, "it's time. Assemble our Enforcer legion and escort the werearmy to the gates of the palace."

"Yes, Council Leader," he says, vanishing in a flash of blue fire.

"I go." Femke comes to my side, hugs me. "I'll see you shortly."

I let her leave without comment as a small group of vampires flicker into shadow and vanish. Sunny remains behind, Frank leading her forces. Sebastian bows over my hand, kissing the back of it, blue eyes mysterious.

"All will be well, Your Highness," he says.

"With your help, I can't believe otherwise," I say.

He winks and leaves me, Alison taking his place. I'm surprised by her sudden bravery, but she hugs me anyway.

Eva Southway has her own agenda, Alison's mental voice reaches me, cold and distant, but clear.

I have no doubt, I send back. *But thank you for the warning.*

Alison curtsies a little before leaving with Sebastian.

Ethpeal and Demetrius join us as Piers leaves with his mother. Her glare at Syd's grandmother and her husband aren't lost on me. When the Southways and their people are gone, I grip Ethpeal's hand in my own.

"She resents you," I say.

The former Enforcer and coven leader snorts. "There's a shocker," she says, sounding so much like her granddaughter we all laugh.

"Have no fear," Demetrius says, loving eyes on his wife. "I'm far more clever than Eva will ever be. Nothing will happen to harm my girl."

Ethpeal pats his cheek, but she's blushing. "Silly man," she says. "I can take care of myself."

I know better than to worry about them, I suppose. But they are family, so I can't help it.

"We have a plan to rescue your grandfather," Ethpeal says. She exchanges a look with her husband who nods to her. "It's risky, but we're pretty sure we can break through Rupe's defenses long enough to reach Oleksander."

I hesitate, heart aching. "And Sage?"

Demetrius's bright blue eyes are sad as he shakes his head. "It's one or the other, I'm afraid."

I squeeze Syd's hand. "Then we go in and save them both by force."

Syd lets out a big gust of air, beaming a smile. "Shall

we join the army?"

I grin back at her. "Nice to be on the other side for once, isn't it?"

She laughs. "Tell me about it."

TWENTY-FOUR

I know these gates well, have stood on both sides of them in my lifetime, as a slave and a princess. The long, winding road beyond leads through the heavy forest and to the palace where my grandfather and my love await rescue.

Syd stands apart, arms crossed over her chest, the cool night air carrying the promise of winter to come. I stay out of the way of Femke, Eva Southway glued to her hip, where the European Leader talks quietly with a large werewolf through the metal bars.

She'll receive no invitation from Caine, forced to assault the palace if she wants to take control of the situation. A heavy shield keeps us out, no matter our plans to enter. I'm hardly surprised Rupe has protected the grounds, though the power he's expending to protect such a large area has to be draining on his energy.

No matter. Let the army sit here and talk all they want. I'm more than willing to leave Femke and Eva here dealing with politics while I find my own way through Rupe's defenses.

Syd's hand hooks my arm as I turn to leave. The large group of vampires, werewolves now loyal to me, and Enforcers wait with growing impatience on the outside of the gate. I avoid eye contact with Piers who stands with his mother's people, Ethpeal and Demetrius also returned to those ranks.

"Tell me you're not thinking of doing what I think you're thinking," she says.

My lips quiver in amusement, pent-up tension working its way through my body as a thrill of excitement. There was a moment, in Wilding Springs, I thought this would all be over quickly, one way or another. I was so wrong. But this time I'm certain. Either Cicero Caine dies today or I do. Either way, it will be over.

"I need the distraction," I say. "All of you, out here, beating your chests and threatening Caine will distract him and Rupe. While I sneak in the back and free Oleksander and Sage."

"At least take some backup." She's going to volunteer—even insist—but I shake my head, pulling away.

"I won't risk others," I say. "I can handle myself. Please, just make sure you're noisy."

Syd grins suddenly, fierce, her own wolf showing, if she had one. "My demon seems to think she knows the perfect deflection," Syd says before pausing, smile failing. "Be careful."

I'm amazed she's letting me go alone. But when I hug her magic with mine, I feel her pride in me, her understanding I need to do this, to see this through without help, if I'm ever going to take my place as ruler of the werenation.

We've both grown up, it appears.

I skirt the edge of the fence, knowing exactly where I'm going. It doesn't cover the entire territory, just about a half mile either way into the trees. The Czar and his Black Souls never felt threatened by other magic races and only erected the barrier to keep out curious normals. And my grandfather continued the tradition.

I know these woods as well as I know myself. I'm just out of range of the coalition forces when I begin to shed my clothing, jogging into the dark, feeling my way along the fence and Rupe's shields. Hopefully, Syd and her demon won't do too much damage, but right now, I'll take all the distraction I can get.

Caine will know I'm coming for him by other means than a frontal assault. The question is, will he guess I'll come alone? I'm about to find out.

My wereshape feels awkward, but I resist falling into full wolf form just yet. My legs are longer this way, my body stronger and I still have complete access to my magic, if not as powerfully. This will do to cover the mile-long run to the palace grounds. If I can get past the shields. This might be a short trip leading me right back to Syd and the others.

The moment I reach the edge of the fence, the protections Rupe's created vanish with the physical barrier. I laugh my werewolf amusement into the darkness. He might want the job, but Rupe is no Liander Belaisle. I should be grateful he's not nearly as foresighted as his old master. When I slip across the border into were territory, I realize the truth of Rupe's little game. He's set up a front, a false wall to fake out the army. Then again, maybe this is a trap set just for me, but he's a fool to let me get closer to him, so I willingly take the bait and begin to run.

They ghost from the darkness around me, their scent welcome, as is their presence. I've missed my little wolf pack, find myself slowing to greet them. The white wolf bows her head to me, pawing at the dirt with her claws, tail swinging behind her. The huge alpha stands at her side, their pack gathered in the gloom behind them.

It's the first time I realize they feel odd to me. Now my full magic is open and available, I realize this pack isn't what they seem. In fact, the white wolf and her alpha aren't real wolves at all, though it takes me a stunned moment to accept it.

"Weres," I growl between my wolf jaws, my wereshape allowing me to speak out loud. "You were werewolves once."

The white yips a bark at me, takes a step forward. No wonder they trail me every time I'm here. The part of them that was human recognized me. Does that mean they, too, retained their humanity like Sage?

Or had it been freed when Syd released them—at the same time she released the rest of the werenation—from the magic of the Black Souls? I stare down into the white wolf's eyes and shudder all over, my fur rippling with understanding. Maybe there was a time they were wolves, lost to the shape they took. But they are now trapped, the people they were, inside the bodies they embraced. Like Sage was.

No, they are much further distant, unable to connect with me mentally. I feel their humanity, though the longer I focus, the closer to the surface their personalities rise and a sick, horrible feeling bubbles in my stomach as I understand who they are.

The alpha barks once, growls as his pack retreats and I no longer have time to focus on the pair of wolves before me. I turn, snarling at the scent I've finally detected, downwind hiding their approach, as six wolves slink from the trees toward me. Not wereshapes, but full wolf forms, and I know them, regardless the bodies they wear.

"Roman." I snap my teeth at the giant timber wolf as he lets out a low howl, head down, fur on end. "And Viveca." She's smaller than her brother, but no less dangerous, yellow eyes full of hatred. Piers let her go once before. I won't allow her or her brother to escape this time.

The rest of this pack are Caine's, I can feel the hint of taint in them, the sorcery that made them even now detectable. Which gives me hope. They have access to their full wolf forms, but their magic must still be restricted thanks to the flaw in their makeup.

I have no such restraints.

My little pack is gone, though the white wolf and the alpha remain with me. As I knew they would. I don't allow another moment to pass, sinking fully into my wolf shape and leaping at Viveca.

Roman tries to block me, but the alpha is on him, the white wolf at his side, and he's forced to fight them off. More wolf bodies flicker among the trees and I realize my little pack hasn't left me after all.

Viveca lunges for my throat, but I'm faster than her, my shoulder hitting hers with my full weight, my magic slamming against her at the same moment. She staggers back away from me, snarling and snapping, only to lunge again. I see my advantage immediately. She's lost in her rage, gone berserk in her need to harm me. All I need to do is maintain my calm and she is mine.

I would love to toy with her, take my time teaching her before I tear her heart out, but I have little time and more important foes to fight. A quick snap with my jaws and her back left hamstring tears, sending her scrambling out of reach with a sharp cry of pain. I crowd her, teeth carving a chunk from her neck before I take out the rest of her back end with a blow to her lower spine. She crumples into the leaves, howling her pain. I shift up and out into wereshape, raising one claw over her as she, too, loses her wolf form and begins to change.

I can have no pity. My claw descends, slicing across her throat, blood gushing from her severed artery and vein, a gasp of lost wind echoing from the top of her open windpipe. She's human again, falling backward from me, eyes huge and full of shock, mouth gaping open while her torn throat geysers a double fountain of blood up and over her body. She collapses to the sound of Roman screaming her name.

A glance up, all the time I have, before her brother leaps for me. But he's forgotten the two he fights, his wolf form gone to wereshape, no match for their tag-team. The white wolf hits him hard in the torso mid-flight, sending him sideways to crash into a tree. The alpha is ready and waiting, his teeth closing around

Roman's face. The crunch of crushing bone rings loud in the sudden silence, the former beta jerking like a broken puppet as the alpha pulps his now human face into unrecognizable meat.

The alpha steps back, panting, jaws dripping blood, as the white wolf lunges in and does to Roman's throat with her teeth what I did to Viveca's with my claws. His blood runs sluggish, his heart already slowed, and it's only a moment before it stops forever.

I spin to check in on my little pack, only to find them standing with us, panting, tails swinging, Caine's weres long gone. I lift my muzzle and howl into the night, the pack joining me, even as a dozen or so werewolves burst through the trees and come to a halt.

I know my father's wereshape. He shifts to human while a surge of hate for him pounds a stake into my chest. "Tell me," I snarl, pointing with my claws at the two wolves who stare up at him, "these aren't who I think they are?" Who I know they are. How did I miss it? Did I simply not want to know the beloved pair weren't dead, but instead lived on in the bodies of wolves? I choke on a sob, fury holding it back.

Raoul won't look at me, or at them. "Your mother and brother are dead to the pack," he says. "So say the law of the werewolves."

TWENTY-FIVE

I leap at my father, but the white wolf puts herself between me and him and I'm forced to retreat. She turns her back on him, facing me, one paw rising to swipe the air. I reach for her, my power engulfing her, feel her own magic dormant inside her.

"Why haven't you woken?" I crouch before her, touching her fur with my hands, wanting to cry but unable to let myself go. I must solve this mystery and understand. "You're free. Why can't you access your magic?"

"They are gone," Raoul says, but I glare at him, a sharp and angry jab of power joining my furious expression and he falls silent.

"Your father is right." Maksym is lucky I don't send him flying. But he is my friend and I am more willing to listen. Sorrow makes his voice quaver. "Olena gave her life—everything she is—to protect you."

I spin on him, temper flaring. Friend or not, I'll kill him if he's deceived me. "You knew?"

He nods sadly, gestures around at the other werewolves watching. "We all did," he said. "It was Oleksander's decision to keep her loss from you. To tell you she was killed instead of this tragedy." His sad gaze falls on the white wolf.

I shake my head, focusing on my mother. Her ears are perked and she's watching me carefully. "Perhaps there was a time she was lost to us," I say. "But they are free, don't you understand?" I think of Sage. But he was never under the control of sorcery when he became a full wolf. He only lost his humanity after Rupe put controls on him. I can't bring myself to believe Sage is gone forever, but can be restored if he is freed. Could it be my mother and brother have simply been in these shapes too long to save them, too?

"Your mother had an idea," Raoul says, voice low and dull and I listen only because I'm trying to think. "That if she could embrace her full wolf form, she could free herself from the Czar's control."

"You had it partially right, *Matinka*," I whisper to her. She barks a soft sound in agreement. "But you needed help, first." I turn to Maks, ignoring my father. "And Danilo?"

"The Czar forced him into this shape," my friend says. "Promised him he would not kill you if your brother agreed to become a mindless animal."

I'm human again, tears squeezing from my eyes, down my cheeks. My nakedness I ignore. My people couldn't care less. I hug the white wolf, her thick fur coarse against my bare skin. The alpha joins us, pressing his wide head against my shoulder until I hug him, too.

"You know the laws, Sharlotta." Raoul's words carry. "No were can take full wolf form and retain their humanity. They are dead to the pack."

I hit him hard with power, slamming him back into a tree. "In case you missed it," I snarl, "they seem to remember me."

He coughs, gasps a breath, but doesn't grow angry. If anything, he sounds resigned. "A dumb animal's recognition," he says.

The white wolf turns toward him and snaps her teeth. I laugh, angry and harsh.

"She seems to disagree." When she faces me again, I meet her gaze. "Mother," I whisper. "Is it you, still, inside?"

She nods, licks my cheek. The feeling of her is growing stronger, as though focus draws her out. I turn to the alpha. "Danilo?"

Another swipe of a tongue before he shakes his heavy head and barks like a happy puppy.

My heart soars. I must find a way to bring them out of their wolf shapes and back to human. But when I try with my own magic, I can't grasp them. It's as though they are there, but behind some kind of shielding. When I probe it, I realize it's their own magic keeping them contained.

"Had you shifted after you were free," I say to them, "you would have had access to your magic. But because you were forced into this shape when the Black Souls still controlled you, the power inside you instead formed a protection around you to keep you safe." The shielding repels me as I try to work my way past my mother's. "We need help with this. And I know the perfect person to ask." I stand, turning my back on my father, facing the werewolves he brought with him. "The old laws are no longer valid," I say. "Revenants are a thing of the past." They murmur, shift on their wereform paws. "The lies and superstitions we were raised on have kept us captive, long after we were freed from the Black Souls." They are paying careful attention. Excellent. Because I'm about to show them something important and I need their focus. I reach for my wolf and embrace her as I finish. "Freedom, true freedom, comes from what we've always been told was impossible." I shift quickly, throwing myself into full wolf shape, listening to their whimpers of shock, how they shiver at the sight of me.

My mind embraces all of theirs, shows them—even

my father—I'm am intact and, better, more powerful than ever before. *We have been denied the truth of our evolution*, I send. *Embrace your wolf and your true power.*

For a long moment, I think I've lost them. And then Maks's magic touches mine and he shifts, releasing a startled yip as he morphs into a tall-shouldered timber wolf.

Charlotte! His mental voice is loud and clear, surging with sudden joy as his wolf body spins in a circle, a dance of utter happiness. *I had no idea.* He sinks to his haunches, tongue lolling out before he snaps his teeth at the watching weres. *Don't be fools*, he sends. *This is amazing!*

They shift almost as one, fear mixed with blind trust rippling outward as their magic wakes fully and washes over me. I laugh as best I can in wolf form, looking up to find only my father has remained in human shape.

I snap my teeth at him and turn my tail. *We go to the palace*, I send to my wolves who respond instantly with eagerness. *And we take back our home.*

They howl, loud and echoing, into the sky. My mother and brother race at my side as I run for the edge of the trees, leaving my father behind.

Let him stay, cling to the old ways. The werenation will evolve. And my people will finally, truly, be free.

TWENTY-SIX

By the time I reach the side yard of the palace, the coalition force is already parked out front, have won through the initial barrier Rupe put up in front of them. Femke still doesn't seem to be in fight mode, but from the tense feel of the standoff, battles could erupt at any moment.

I'll leave it to them, though I wonder when Syd's distraction will come into play. Curious, I reach out to her and feel her immediately.

Let me know when you're in position, she sends.

You've been waiting for me? Probably an excellent idea and something I should have thought of.

Of course, she sends. *We all have.* She pauses. *Something's changed.*

I made a discovery. I send her happy energy so she

knows I'm fine. *I'll need your help with it later. For now, consider me in position.* I stop at the edge of the trees to observe. Planning to go in the back, through my room, as long as Rupe has made the same mistake with the protections around the palace as he did the fence. As long as he's only shielding the front of the building, I should be able to sneak in. And considering the massive size of the palace, I have to believe his power isn't enough to protect all of it. *Is Femke ready?*

She is. Syd leaves me a moment then returns. *Eva and her people have been holding off the sorcerers and your people remaining don't seem to want to fight. I have a feeling this is going to be quick and dirty and won't end well for Rupe.*

My lips lift, a wolf growl escaping. *What a shame. Shall we begin?*

I leap out of the trees, in a dead run, heading across the side yard for the back of the palace just as a huge column of fire erupts to fill the front lawn with flame. The sky is so bright I have to squint, while the pounding weight of sorcery leaves the surrounds of the palace and diverts forward, to Syd's show of temper.

Perfect, I send to her. Mission accomplished. The few wereguards patrolling the side of the palace leap into action, running for the front lawn, leaving my path wide open. I feel the edge of the shielding brush past on my left and almost howl my excitement I was right about Rupe's inexperience and inability to protect the entire place. I'm inside the grounds and nothing can keep me from Caine now.

I shift into wereshape to climb the trellis, my fellow werewolves following suit. I look down to find my mother and brother circling a moment before they run back the way they came. I don't care if they are retreating. I'm more than happy to tackle this and keep them safe.

The werenation has let them down long enough.

My room is dark and quiet, suddenly filled with panting, angry werewolves. I creep to the door and open to my wolf, her senses reaching out into the hallway. Rupe is even more of a fool than I thought. He's closed off the front of the palace, but failed to block my power within, as he did at the castle where Andre tortured me. Perhaps this place really is too big for such protections. Or maybe he's chosen to instead only shore up the throne room. There's only one way to find out.

The hall is as dark and quiet as my room. I gesture to the weres with me to follow, feeling them fan out behind me. A flicker of motion ahead becomes two wereguards, both of whom who immediately morph into wereshape upon seeing me and join my ranks.

I feel their minds, the hints of the coercion that bound them burning away and offer my power in return. They accept it willingly as we descend the broad staircase to the vast foyer.

Never has this gaudy and over-gilded space been so

beautiful to me. I step down onto the cold floor, nose lifting as I sniff the air to catch the scents I seek. Caine's burns at me, pulling me to the right toward the throne room, and I follow eagerly, trusting the rest of my weres to guard my back.

Light shines through the large windows, casting across the floor from behind me, throwing my shadow ahead. Blue fire mixed with rainbow light and the flares of white spirit magic thud against the front of the palace. The fight Syd set off is going strong. I focus on the two wereguards standing at the throne room doors, maintaining my aggressive forward pace. They seem stunned, dazed almost. When I reach out to their minds, I realize why. I was right about the protections Rupe was able to manage. These two stand just outside the thick, black shielding, their coercion still in place, but held almost in stasis as the shields feed from them.

I free the pair with a jerk of my wolf's energy, the two large guards stumbling forward, finally recognizing me. I snap at them, but not in anger, and they shift to join me, wereforms taking over as their fury surges. Awake and aware, they know what they've been forced to do, who they've been put here to protect.

Frustration burns tiny holes in my resolve as I come to a halt at the entry to the throne room. I touch the edge of the shielding, transparent until my fingers slide over it and the thick, black goo of it sucks at my claws. I pull away with a hiss of disgust, glaring down the length of the deep purple carpet to the scene unfolding near the throne dais.

I recognize my grandfather's kneeling shape, his silver head turned to look back over his shoulder at me. I can't make out his expression, nor feel him through the wards around the room. The other man crouched by the throne I know even better, my heart constricting at the sight of Sage, clearly still lost to the animal he's become thanks to sorcery as he shakes his head and paces back and forth like a chained lion.

Power pushes against my back as the front door slams open and a wave of magic users storms through. I turn and gesture at Syd who's in the front line, and she hurries toward me at a fast trot. Femke joins her, Piers and her grandmother at her side, as I point at the blocked way before me.

"If you would," I growl, staring at Caine who lounges on the throne of my grandfather like he's not about to have his ass handed to him. He even has the balls to wave at me, the remains of his pack hovering around him and a double line of coerced wereguards standing at attention. There's no sign of Rupe, but he has to be here, he and his sorcerer friends, in order for this barrier to stand.

Syd's rainbow power cuts through the shields and they sigh apart, crumbling to dust before disappearing. She turns and holds out one hand toward the throne room with a wicked smile.

"After you, Your Highness."

I stride down the carpet toward the throne, ignoring the waking wereguards who shake their heads and stare around in disbelief and growing anger. Caine is so close I can taste him in the back of my throat, smell the stench of him. Soon I will have his blood on my teeth and this will all be over.

"Stop!" He stands abruptly, hands out, chest bare under the heavy robe he wears open to expose his heavily tattooed skin. Caine grins at me and I wonder if he's gone mad to think he can order me to do anything.

One of his werewolves lunges forward and grasps my grandfather, pulling his chained form sideways, claws at Oleksander's throat. Two others pin Sage down while my love howls like a wild animal for his freedom.

"That's close enough." Caine's grin is feral. Does he really think this will stop me? I'm surrounded by magic, powerful people who can kill him and his pack in a heartbeat. I feel suddenly sorry for this man and the delusions ruling him, most likely fed to him by Rupe. "Your precious grandfather and your human pet have been waiting for you, princess."

Syd's power is building next to me, but I wave her off and take a step forward. "It's over, Caine." I half turn, look behind me at the Enforcers, vampires, werewolves and sorcerers ready to strike him down at the least provocation. "Release them and I might be merciful."

Caine laughs. It's genuine amusement, doubling him over as he clutches his naked waist. When he sobers, his face alters into spiteful hate, a smile still on his lips.

"You hear that, Rupe?" Caine opens both arms, self-assurance making me nervous. "I suppose we should surrender then, shouldn't we?"

Rupe emerges from behind the throne, a line of sorcerers coming with him. There are more than I expected, almost twenty as I count, their number climbing as Rupe joins Caine on the throne dais. I hear the throne room doors slam shut and turn to see more sorcerers forming a wall between us and escape.

TWENTY-SEVEN

A trap? It's my turn to laugh.

"This is supposed to impress me?" I shake my head, my wereform not allowing a full smile as I go on. "You do realize I have sorcerers of my own with me."

Caine lurches down the first step, face morphing to wereshape. "You're too late to stop us," he snarls. "I am the one true king!" His pack shift nervously, and I wonder if he's lost his mind and their loyalty.

Rupe's grin is as evil, his eyes bulging as he focuses on Syd. As he speaks, I feel the thread of power between him and Caine and realize it's not the Californian leader who has cracked.

"I hoped you'd come." Rupe is clearly broken inside, his mind gone, though what caused the snap I have no idea. He was deluded and had a God complex the last time we met, but he wasn't insane. Not that he showed me. The sorcerer who stands on the dais is no longer fully in control of his faculties.

Though he is, it seems, of his power. I feel it crush down on me, try to take me over again. But Syd is faster, her rainbow maji magic slicing through the rope of black he throws at me and mine.

Like this. She shows me what she's done, how her power made a barrier. I try to emulate her, but without access to my sorcery, I fail.

I can't, I send. *I can use the elemental magic of the witches and the demon power, but I have no access.* I fumble at my own magic with growing frustration.

Sorcery isn't in you, she sends. *It is you.*

She leaves me to ponder that as she speaks.

"You're done, Rupe." Syd sounds sad mixed with angry. "I don't want to kill you, but I will if you make me."

He thumbs his nose at her, sticking out his tongue like a child even as the sorcery encasing the throne room tightens a notch. I feel darkness push outward, know the Steam Union are fighting him, but their number is far less than Rupe's followers. Eva and her dozen or so members are hard-pressed to combat the now fifty odd Rupe has at his command.

This trap might not be so ludicrous after all.

"Caine was right about one thing," Rupe says, hands jerking at the collar of his shirt. A bite mark scores his flesh, oozing blood, unnoticed against the black fabric until now. "But he was wrong about being king. I claim the throne of the werenation!"

Caine spins on him, snarling, crouching as he slips into wereshape. "That wasn't our agreement." Has he broken free of Rupe's influence, or did the insane sorcerer release him? I have no way of knowing, but Caine suddenly is open to me, no longer shrouded by the dark sorcery binding him to Rupe. He tries to approach the throne, but is held back by a wall of darkness that ripples when he hits it.

The whole room sways as the werewolves are drawn into the power Rupe siphons, myself included. Syd tries to block him again, but I feel the pathways he spoke of, the old ones of my birth that tie me still to the Black Souls, open to the sorcerer. My power goes to him without a fight. I feel the pressure of the coercion field then, whispering to me, that I'm surrounded by enemies, the ones I came with here to enslave me. My only hope is with my wereking, Caine and the lord of all, Rupe. It would be so easy to fall, to allow these thoughts to win. But I am too far past the truth to let such magic defeat me.

The field isn't strong enough to survive my determination. As I shake off the influence, I look around at my people, gazing with glazed eyes at the throne. Are we that weak minded, to be controlled by a film of magic? A glance at the sorcerers Rupe brought tells me we're not the only ones he is stealing energy from, and realize the coercion field is merely a side-event to Rupe's true intent.

Rupe sits slowly as his power increases, a huge, scary smile on his face. "All hail the wereking!"

Again, he crushes down on me, almost driving me to my knees, though his slippery attempt to take my mind fails. Syd grapples with him, but with his own sorcery and the power he's stealing, pushes her back.

Her eyes meet mine. *He can't be infected, right?*

I don't know. It shouldn't be possible, but who knows?

Her blue gaze bubbles with anxiety. *I can't free you*, she sends. *You're going to have to learn to do it yourself.* She shows me a dark flower, the blossom beneath her. I've heard her describe it that way before, but never experienced it, at least not like this. *You see it?*

I do. I feel it, too. But when I try to create the same in me, my sorcery slips out of my control.

The power is you, Syd sends, repeating herself, and as Rupe crushes down harder on me, I finally understand. I'm reaching for something I already have, trying to find a magic right here, and in searching am missing the point. There's nothing to find. Only something to call on.

My wolf chuffs as she shifts inside me, magic gaping and a rush of black power surges outward. The controls

Rupe holds over me shatter and fall away as dark magic pools at my feet, wavering like wind-swept grass.

Rupe's eyes bulge as he glares at me, Syd's voice in my head ringing like a battle cry. *Well done!*

I take a step forward, my sorcery crawling around me as I glance from side to side at the people who have come to fight. The witches, vampires and weres will have no protection, can serve as a source of power to Rupe if this goes on much longer. I must act before they can be harmed.

This is my war to win.

I take another step forward. "In case you weren't aware," I snarl, "you're in my seat."

Rupe's narrowed eyes focus on me, his sorcery pushing against me, burrowing through to seek out the controls he's lost. My wolf snaps at him and sends him running. Maybe I can force him to focus on me, to weaken his concentration and give the Steam Union a chance.

I don't get a chance to find out if my plan will work. Caine howls in anger and throws himself at the shield protecting his former ally, bouncing away from it, sideways, toward Sage. My love screams in protest, his wolf body altering to wereshape as he flings himself at Caine. The two meet in mid-air, the thunderous crash of their coming together echoing through the throne room as their magic impacts at the same time.

Now! I send the thought to Syd, but she's already acting, as are the Steam Union. I crouch and hurry forward, staying low and out of the way, as Syd's magic batters the shielding around the throne. The were holding my grandfather is so stunned by the unfolding events, he barely registers my attack as I take him out with a solid blow to the side of his head. Oleksander's power is blunted, I feel sorcery controlling him, so I use my own to shatter his chains and pull him out of the way, into the arms of waiting Gwendolyn and Finlay, Maks and Isabelle tight on their heels.

When I turn back, it's to the sight of Sage pinned to the carpet, Caine's wolf jaws descending to my love's throat. I have no time to reach them, to save Sage. Caine was right after all.

I'm too late.

Sage! I scream in his mind, my magic the only part of me fast enough to close the distance, to show him what I've uncovered, discovered about myself, my sorcery. And in the split second between his coming death and his last moment of life, Sage's mind breaks through the controls, seizing his dark power, and I feel him return to me.

Caine's teeth close on empty air as Sage, human and thinking again, does the unexpected. He scoots sideways, out from under Caine's body, twisting as he goes, legs locking around his opponent's. I've seen this move, had Sage use it on me before in the dojo. Only this isn't some marital arts training session, it's life and death. And, I know Caine doesn't stand a chance against this maneuver, now that Sage is back.

I'm not too late after all.

It's Caine's turn to howl as Sage strikes, extended claws slicing through the Californian's shoulder and neck while a mist of black undulates beneath them, Sage's sorcery drawing on Caine's strength. Panting and still struggling despite the loss of blood, Caine reverts to human while Sage does the same.

"No!" Rupe's scream takes my attention from my love and his success, to Syd pushing with relentless purpose through the shielding protecting the sorcerer. I've never seen her look so determined, or so full of the need to kill. The werewolves of my nation are falling to their knees as the coercive field fails. Eyes no longer glazed, they remain unable to fight, their very lives sucked away by Rupe, as are the sorcerers he made part of his trap. I focus on my sorcery, on the connection he has to all of them, and feel the embedded thread of darkness running under the floor of the throne room. It has many branches, like the sickening tentacles of a mythical kraken, drawing out the power of those it's tied to. I follow it back to the root, to the edge of the shield Syd forces herself against, and link with her.

She sees what I've discovered the moment our minds touch and, with my power tied to hers, slashes outward with the power of the maji, cutting the cord.

The whole room sighs, bodies hitting the floor, the sudden release and recoil of their magic sending the werewolves down, but the sorcerers flying backward.

Rupe's scream of denial echoes in the huge room as he claws at the air around him, as though trying to pull the threads back. His body begins to morph into wereform, but I know immediately something is wrong with his transformation. Misshapen and incomplete, his limbs seem oddly bent, patches of baldness on his exposed flesh showing diseased skin. He leaps from the throne, personal wards still in place, still strong, though weakening now he has no one to feed them, shifting back and forth between horribly mutated werewolf and mad human.

The pressure is so powerful I clamp my hands over my ears, my fellow weres doing the same. Something must give or we will all rupture from the intensity of the two magicks coming together.

It's Rupe's that breaks, snapping back from Syd like a bungee cord severing under too much weight. She staggers, enough time for Rupe to spin, red face still clutched in madness, and run behind the throne. She runs after him, but I can feel his power sucking at the energy in the room and know he's already gone.

The sorcerers he brought with him lay scattered, mostly unconscious, around the throne room. I cannot bring myself to feel sympathy for them as the werewolves of my pack begin to round them up.

I turn to run to Sage, relief making me giddy. And gasp as his smiling face turns to me, not seeing the hate in Caine as the injured Californian rises and lunges for my love.

I'm already throwing power at Caine, but Sage is in the way and I can't risk hurting him. Too late, this time, I'm out of position and Sage is too slow to spin at the sound of Caine rising. Time slows. I'm locked in a well of inching seconds. Sage turning, Caine lashing out with sharp claws, the strength of the blow surely enough to remove my love's head from his shoulders.

Three shapes—one white, one gray and a third black—streak across the carpet. The black wolf is fastest, slamming between Sage and Caine. Time snaps back into motion and I'm running already, grasping for Sage, shoving him out of the way, my own claws striking, taking Caine across the face with one paw, the other embedding itself up under his ribcage to grip his heart.

He gapes at me as I jerk the pumping muscle free and hold it in front of his dying eyes. He shifts to human, falling at my feet, blood pooling around my paws, his heart jerking two more beats in my hand before falling silent.

I look down, at the white wolf who is my mother, the gray who is my brother. I realize the third, the black shape who saved Sage, now lying in a river of running blood with his body cut almost in half, is my father.

I fall to my knees at his side, the white wolf whimpering as she licks his face. Raoul is human again, but when I reach for him with magic, I feel his wolf dying, unable to heal the massive injury. I'm crying, clutching at him, pushing power into him, but it's not enough, will never be enough.

It's only the power of the wolf that keeps him awake, aware, as he looks into my eyes. My grandfather joins me, kissing his son, weeping openly while Raoul tries to speak.

"Olena," his voice is a wet, bubbling sound as his lungs fill with blood. "I did as you asked. Everything I did, I did to protect our children." He meets my eyes. "Including taking the first chance I had to free Charlotte."

Free me? And then, I understand, and I'm sobbing, a broken-hearted little girl who blamed her father for the wrong thing. I thought him a coward, without *сан*. But Raoul Moreau gave up his own honor in order to align me with Syd, to force me to bond with her.

"How did you know?" I bend over my dying father, tears mingling with his blood.

"No one ever," he coughs, gasps, "stood against the Dumonts. Until her." He twitches, the light in his eyes dimming. "If anyone could free you, it was Sydlynn. And her family. At least you would be with those of honor."

I bow my head, heart squeezing tight with regret. So long I blamed him, held him in scorn. But he did what he did to save me.

Breath bubbles heavily in his chest. A normal would be dead by now. Though we've had our differences, and I've doubted his courage, my father saved me the only way he knew how. And now, he's given his life to save my love when he could have let Sage die. For that, I will always be grateful. As I must be grateful I at least have a chance to say goodbye.

The wolf in me is that practical.

My father's fingers rise, run through my mother's fur, a tiny smile on his lips and love in his eyes. And then, his gaze glazes over and Raoul Moreau dies while the werewolves in the room howl over his loss.

TWENTY-EIGHT

I feel my grandfather stir next to me, turn to embrace him. He's still Oleksander, though he's lost weight from his time in captivity and I can only assume Caine and Rupe have treated him badly.

When I pull away, he touches my face with gentle, giant hands, weeping openly. "My darling Sharlotta," he whispers.

The white wolf who is my mother barks sharply at him. Oleksander looks up, stares at her with sadness. "Forgive me," he says. "If you are still there, Olena, I beg of you to forgive me."

She tilts her head to the side, ears perked.

"Grandfather," I say. "I think there's a way to make it right."

He doesn't argue with me, debate werelaw as he once may have. Instead, he hugs me and kisses me before nodding. "The days of the old laws no longer serve us," he says, sounding old and tired. He releases me, slowly standing from the remains of his fallen son and turning to face the assembled magic users. I stand with him, the two wolves at my feet, Sage standing back, though I long to have him next to me.

I've almost forgotten those who came to help us and meet Femke's eyes as my grandfather's booming voice demands attention.

"There is a time and a place for everything," he said, deep voice sad but strong. "And though her actions once went against the laws of our people, she has proved to be the very were we need to lead us." He releases me, bowing to me as the rest of the werenation bows in response. My entire body tenses as they fall to their knees and lower their heads. "I am abdicating the throne," Oleksander says before I can choke out a word to stop him, "a throne stolen from me, and won back for our people by your princess, your future queen." The world is closing in around me and though I knew this could be the end result, I didn't expect it to happen now, here, while my hands and knees are wet with my father's blood and the entirety of magickdom seems to stare in wonder.

Oleksander has no qualms, however. He salutes. "All hail Sharlotta Moreau, ruler of the werenation."

I accept their roar of answer, resolute as the vampires, witches and Steam Union join in the happy cry. But I can't forget who brought me here, to this moment. I turn to find Sage watching me with empty eyes.

I reach for him with my magic, but he blocks me with his. And then I'm swept into the arms of countless werewolves, embraced and celebrated while all I want to do is deny them, reject the responsibility, go to Sage.

Maks finally sets me down as Femke approaches, smiling. "It is our great honor to see you take the throne," she says. "Congratulations, Princess Sharlotta."

I'm numb, but I nod to her anyway. I just need a moment alone with Sage right now, but I guess I'm going to have to wait.

Though I expected less from her, Eva Southway joins Femke in shaking my hand.

"I'd like to offer support in the future." I'm shocked at her offer, frankly. She's shown me little but disdain and opposition since we met. Perhaps my impending change of status influences her. "So this can never happen again."

"If that support," I say, "is to teach werewolves to use their sorcery, your help is welcome."

She seems startled herself. But I've already worked it out in my head, long before she brought it up, shortly after Syd showed me what to do. We have to be our own people, with our own protections. And to do that, we have to not only embrace change, but willingly discard our beliefs while realizing our full potential.

We'll be working on that for a long time to come.

"An excellent idea." Syd chooses that moment to return, cranky and touchy. She pushes herself between Eva and me, bristling with argumentative energy. "Don't you think?"

Eva accepts the conditions graciously. "I take it Rupe is gone?"

Syd spins on me, anger cracking around her. "I don't want to talk about it." Her eyes fall on my father and all the rage runs out of her. She cups both hands over her mouth, gaze lifting to mine, full of tears. I don't give her a chance to say a word, hugging her instead.

"All's well," I say, choking up again at the memory of what my father did for me, "that ends well."

She nods and lets me go, both of us watching as four wereguards gather up the remains of Raoul Moreau and carry him away.

My anger smothers sadness as Maks and Isabelle, aided by Gwen and Finlay, herd the last of Caine's pack into a knot of misery and force them to face me. My power crackles with the need to hurt them, to punish them, but as I open my mouth to snap orders to have them imprisoned, Sage practically leaps between them and me, face set and determined.

"I take responsibility for these werewolves," he says.

223

I gape, anger tempered, but still there, now aimed at him, though I have no idea what he has in mind.

Sage, I send, desperation in my mind. I need him to distance himself from them, not claim allegiance. Especially if he's to be with me. *What are you doing?*

Silence is my answer.

"They are enemies of the werenation," I say out loud.

"Led by someone who knew only darkness," Sage says. He turns and the gathered Californian pack nods at him. It's true, they seem less aggressive and more shaken by the death of their leader, anxious even. Not one of them feels even remotely eager to take up their leader's fight. "Council Leader Svennson." Sage addresses Femke directly, cutting me out of the conversation. It stings, but I let him say his piece. "We would ask you to acknowledge us as true werewolves and free us from the fear of prosecution."

Femke glances at me and back again. "The Witch Council accepts you are no danger, not revenants, though it is up to the werenation to declare your pardon."

Sea green eyes meet mine. "Do we have it?"

My love. My mental voice is a wail, my wolf whimpering at him.

Charlie, Sage answers, his own tone heavy and dark. *I love you. But feel around you.* I do, knowing what I'll sense. The animosity of my people, the disgust and hatred for him, no matter the proof he's no threat to us. *They won't accept me. They won't accept us.* Is he referring to him and me or to the pack now hunkering around him? It doesn't matter, I suppose. *I know you would go against your people to keep us together.* Defeat flavors his mental voice. *But I can't let you give up the life you were meant for. Not now, not when they need you more than ever.*

We can find a way, I send, my need for him an ache I know I'll carry with me the rest of my lonely life if he leaves me.

His beautiful eyes are shadowed. *You are my heart and soul*, he sends, soft, full of grief. *And I'm asking you to please let me go.*

My voice will crack if I speak out loud, but I must. The gathering watches, waiting for my response to his question. How can I just release him now? He's not thinking straight.

Then again, neither am I.

Charlie. Sage's mind hugs mine, his wolf proud and strong though hurting as much as mine. *Princess Sharlotta. You were right all along. It's time to say goodbye.*

I nod at last though my wolf fights me, chest tight with emotion. I'll find him later, talk him out of this. For now, he can have this victory. No matter my resolve, I find I have to clear my throat before I speak. "You have proven you are true werewolves, not the revenants our people fear." My jaw tightens against my need to hug Sage, to pull him aside and have a more private conversation. "But that doesn't erase their traitorous actions. They conspired to remove Oleksander from the throne, to turn you into a revenant, knowing it would mean your death."

"Your pardon," one of the weres speaks up, a slim woman covered in tattoos with three giant rings in one ear but a serious, even professional, demeanor. "We were only following the orders of our pack leader. And there were those of us," nods from the group as she speaks, "who spoke out against this plan."

In human law, following orders isn't a defense. But in pack law... without the pack, a werewolf is nothing. I ponder a moment, wondering if I let them go if they will even be accepted by the rest of the werenation, no matter the pardon I've granted. Chances are, I'll be dooming them to a life outside the full pack.

"What is your name?" I gesture at the werewoman who spoke up.

"Nina Dillon," she says, still firm but calm. She feels steady, trustworthy.

"You will accept this were as your leader, Nina?" Perhaps I can encourage the pack themselves to reject Sage.

But she nods, taking a step closer to him. "We've learned safety in numbers," she says. "And I will accept his leadership for now." She shrugs, the rest bobbing their heads in agreement. "At least until we can settle it among ourselves."

In true werewolf fashion. My last hope is gone.

Sage's gaze doesn't judge me, but he isn't friendly, either. "I will lead them and guide them," he says. "And you have my word they will never harm anyone again."

Give him this. Syd's voice is soft in my head. *He's earned it.*

I want him with me. My own weeps to her.

I know, she sends. *But he's made his choice. And you have a throne to sit on.*

She's right and he is, too. I should fight for him, to keep him here with me, but I can't make him do anything. Wouldn't want to.

"Granted," I say, my lips moving though I feel frozen with grief. "Be free, Sage America."

When he turns to go, I gasp a breath. I didn't expect him to go now, without a word. I reach for his mind, to beg him to return, to talk this through further.

I have to go, he sends, cutting me off. *Before I ruin everything by changing my mind.*

I could pull him back, weep at his feet, kiss and hold him. I know I could make him stay. But I'm held back by my pride and the watchful gazes of all assembled, forced to simply stand there and let the love of my life leave me.

I won't give up on him. Once he's settled, I'll find him, talk it through. Convince the werenation to accept his pack. Surely, I can convince him to come back to me.

The white wolf pushes her nose into my hand, startling me. I look down into her eyes, emotions jerked from the loss of Sage to the hope of my mother's return. My hands grasp for Syd, lips barely able to force out the words.

"Can you restore them?"

I worry, tossed between fear she can't and excitement she can, when I watch Syd study them, Femke beside her, Eva joining the investigation as the three powerful magic users examine my mother and brother. Could a part of my mother and brother always be lost? They had both been trapped in wolf shape for so long.

No matter. Whatever the outcome, I have them back in my lives, even if they remain wolves forever.

The moment Syd sighs a happy "ah-ha!" with a snap of her fingers, I beam a smile, discarding my stoic need to accept the best I can get. I barely have time to draw a breath before my mother's white wolf shape shifts upward and she's human again. She totters on her feet, long years balanced on four feet obviously shaking her equilibrium. I grasp her hands, holding her steady, staring into her eyes, and seeing the woman I remember stare back at me.

I had nothing to fear. She smiles at me, shaky, her eyes that I share brimming with tears before she stumbles forward and hugs me tight.

"Sharlotta," she whispers. "My darling girl, thank

you."

Danilo bursts into human shape with a roar of joy and hugs Syd, nakedness ignored, though my friend is blushing and pushing him off before long.

Thank you. My magic hugs her as my family embraces me, the loss of my father a keen blade in my heart.

You, Syd sends, mental voice full of love, *are very welcome. And finally free.*

Not really. But I'll put my duty before my heart, especially now. My people need me more than ever, and having my mother and brother back fills the gap Sage's departure left behind.

I'll cry over him later. For now, I step away from my family and accept the cheering welcome of my people as I turn and ascend the steps to the throne, spinning and slowly lowering myself to its seat.

TWENTY-NINE

I stare at my reflection, touch my blonde hair. It was an easy enough thing to strip the black dye from it, even encourage growth, as it turns out. I shake it out over my shoulders, long and thick again. I missed it.

So odd the things that matter to me now.

A cold breeze washes in through my window, ruffling the gauzy curtains of my quarters. It's really too late in the season to have them open, the chill of winter less a hint and more a promise, but the fresh air helps me think.

It's hard for me to believe it's only been two weeks since the fall of Caine and the disappearance of Rupe. My fingers trace over the golden tiara resting in an ornate wooden box on my dressing table. This crown belongs to a princess, something I won't be much longer.

I sigh and stand, walking to my wardrobe to dress. The palace still feels like sorcery, but for a good reason this time. The Steam Union made short work of cleaning up the rogue practitioners Rupe left behind, their laws kicking in when the defeat of Caine and Rupe ended the need for the coalition.

At least we have his people here and will be able to question the sorcerers who Rupe abandoned. Tallah's speculation about the state of what remains of the Brotherhood will likely be confirmed by their testimony.

One shaking young man with red hair and far too many freckles told Eva as much in a trembling voice. "Our master has left us," he wailed, clutching at her as though she would save him. "We thought Rupe would be our salvation." The young man wept into his hands. "We are lost."

Happy news that the Brotherhood is in such a state, even now. But I'll need both Belaisle's and Rupe's heads—bodies optional—in my presence before I'll believe this is over.

I shake out the white dress I'm to wear, sinking to the soft mattress of my bed. I may have sat a symbolic moment on the werethrone, but tonight is the real deal, the night I accept the crown and take rule of my people. I let the silky material fall into my lap, biting my lip to keep the almost constant threat of tears from bursting out of me.

Here I am, focused on the future, or trying to, when it's the last thing I want to do. Running the events of the last few days over in my head helps a bit, but every time I skim near two weeks ago, a choking weight threatens to close my throat.

He left me. Went with what remains of Caine's pack, back to America the night of our victory and I haven't heard from him since. Yes, I've been trapped by the circumstances of my position since the throne room was cleared and Oleksander made his fateful speech. And Sage was right about how the werenation feels about him and the others, Caine's former pack. I've heard whispers since, even a few openly challenging remarks I've quickly squashed. The resentment of my people toward the new breed of our race hasn't diminished in the past fourteen days, nor would I expect it to. It may take years for them to learn to accept our people are no longer bound by the superstitions and fears ingrained in us by the Black Souls.

But I expected more from Sage, a battle to stay with me, if nothing else. While I understand his desire to protect me, it's not fair we've finally won, come so far, only to be torn apart by the same old politics. Especially after our conversation on the roof at Oxford. I thought he understood I'd make sure we could be together.

Have the controls Rupe had over him changed Sage somehow? Or is he just tired of the politics, the deceptions, the ways of the werenation?

Tired of me.

No matter his reasons, he is gone, and I'm left here, alone, being pushed toward a future I wish I could stop, but one rushing toward me with the elemental power of a rising tide.

I try not to feel bitter as I stand and slide into the dress. Bitter that my mother and brother have been welcomed home without question, but Sage is still an outcast. Though I suppose it's logical and practical in the way of wolves. Both Mother and Danilo are heroes of our people and have been for decades. Their return has been hailed as miraculous, the fact of their entrapment not even discussed, especially when they joined me in teaching the werenation to take full wolf shape and free the last of their power.

It's not lost on me they are now much like Sage, those who judge and disown him. The last trace of their old prejudice remains and I wonder how long it will take to wear away. Maybe sooner rather than later? It's the human in my people keeping them from accepting Sage and the California pack. Maybe there is hope, once the last of the werenation is woken from their magical suppression and embraces our destiny.

The satin feels like steel suddenly, binding me, holding me in place. But I must continue, go on, endure. Too many people have sacrificed to put me here, tonight, so near the throne I can taste the weight of my impending rule.

And not the least of those, my father. My hands crumple fistfuls of fabric and I hang my head a moment, letting the last of my guilt over judging him wash clean. Yes, I stood at his funeral pyre and held my mother's hand, my brother's on the other side, watched as my grandfather lit the decorated body with a blazing torch. Yes, I endured the sympathies of the gathered leaders, the werenation who loved him even more, loved me and my family now the truth of Raoul's sacrifice has been made clear. That of any werewolf, it was he who gave us our freedom, who led me to Syd and to this moment.

And it is his heroism that has thrust me even closer to taking the throne. The Moreau family, long adored and looked upon as the leaders of our werenation, have been forever immortalized thanks to the selfless act of my father who chose a life of exile and shame to save us all.

I force a smile past the glittering tears on my cheeks as I look up at myself. Both hands smooth the sides of my dress before wiping away the moisture on my cheeks. I've already cried many tears over my loss, not just of my father, but of all that time wasted, time I could have spent loving and trusting him.

The werewoman in the mirror sighs out the last of her grief at the sight of herself, the satin sheath hugging non-existent curves. I'm thin, too bony. There's so little time to eat, so much to do. The past two weeks have flown by and I can barely remember any of it. My hands slide over my arms. It's been wonderful reconnecting with my brother and my mother. Especially Danilo. Mother is a memory newly refreshed, a face and heart long gone from me. But my brother's presence I have missed desperately.

He seems to feel the same. We've spent every moment possible together and I've leaned heavily on him since Oleksander's announcement.

"You'll make a wonderful queen," my brother told me last night, while I paced in a weak moment of panic. I've been suffering episodes of fear, when I have time to stop and realize I'm about to take the throne. Danilo's dark eyes are our father's and remind me of Raoul's sacrifice. "Anything you need, Sharlotta. You know I'm here for you."

"I need," I said, sinking down beside him, "to find a way to make this go away." I smile at him, trembling lips traitors. I hate to show weakness to my brother, but he understood. He always has. Danilo leaned forward and hugged me, magic touching mine with the strength I remember, his hero's heart as big and supportive as ever.

"I'm sorry you're so unhappy, my sister." He let me go, his own face sad. "In this time of victory, there is so much I wish was different."

"I'll manage." The Moreau pride woke then, and I found a real smile to share with him.

My brother didn't say anything, simply kissed me and left me alone, his head bowed as he departed. I miss him even now as I remember, and wonder how much pain he carries. My questions about what he remembers from his time as a full wolf have gone unanswered, though the sorrow in both his and my mother's eyes when I've gently inquired told me their journey has been just as painful as mine.

My hands fall to my sides, biceps thin and lean. I frown at my physique, a distraction from my thoughts, focusing on the trivial to keep me centered. My reduced muscle flexes as I make a fist. I need to find time to work out and build my lost muscle back. Which makes me think of Sage.

Again. I have a feeling this cycle will go on for a very long time.

I heard from Tallah this morning, the werewolves arriving safely in her territory.

"I'll keep an eye on him for you," she said as I thanked her for letting me know. At least I don't have to worry if she's going to watch over him. I just hope Sage doesn't alienate her out of some misguided sense of lone wolfness. He'll need a friend or two while he figures things out. At least Nina seems to support him and, from my brief contact with her, seems level headed and confident. A likely mate, perhaps.

I clench my fists against such a thought and snarl at

my reflection.

I should be the one helping him. Anger spits sparks inside me as I push at the heavy chair in front of my dressing table, knocking it into the wall. But temper won't help me. I'm here, trapped in this life. I can't let my people down now.

My hair sticks with static to my hands as I wind it back into a bun. I could have help, maids to assist, but I want to do this alone. I do manage a grin as I think of how pissed off Erica must have been to find out Sage and the others were making North America their home. Syd gave me the smug impression it took her, Femke and, surprisingly, Eva, to convince her, but I have no doubt it was mostly Syd. Of course, that knowledge is counterbalanced by the expected lack of action against the Dumonts. Why am I not surprised to hear there was no punishment waiting for them at home, no reprimand? That Erica simply ignored their involvement in this debacle and allowed business as usual?

All is well. Andre and I have an appointment. I'm content to wait to keep it.

My fingers fumble as I stab myself with a bobby pin. I let my hands fall to my lap, hair tumbling down in waves and think of Zoe Helios. I might not have much freedom once I'm on the throne, at least to act as an individual. But I really need to track that girl down and find out what else she knows. Having access to an Oracle might make all the difference the next time trouble rolls around.

I'm not foolish enough to think we're free and clear. But with the Steam Union actually on our side, Eva and her people accepting the werenation finally as our own people as a race and not one to be looked down on or feared, maybe we can make enough progress when the next disaster hits, we'll be ready.

Piers refused to rejoin his mother, the only other dark mark on our victory, and I know it has to be eating Eva up. Maybe his defection has forced her to face the flaws in her leadership. Though I wonder what my sorcerer friend will do without his own particular pack.

"I'll be fine," he informed me this afternoon over lunch, gray eyes sparkling. "I have some things to look into, my own plans that Mum and the others don't need to know about."

"What about your werefriend?" I prodded him with my fork.

"All in good time," he said before kissing me and leaving me, too.

They all left, of course, Syd and Femke and the vampires, taking most of the disruption with them. It's taken two weeks to clean up the mess, to return the palace to normal. I miss my friends already, though I'll see them shortly, downstairs, when I take the throne.

My body shudders against the thought.

A soft knock at the door pushes me to my feet. I

know it's her before I pull the portal open, already reaching for Syd. She hugs me and then slips inside my room, turning to face me as I close the door behind her.

"You're sure about this?" Leave it to Syd to push my waterworks button. I shake my head, lips tight against the need to cry.

She sighs and flops down onto the bed. "Of all people," she says. "Charlotte, if you don't want the throne, don't take it."

"Of all people," I repeat. "You know I have to."

We stare at our hands in silence, equally glum.

"Sorry," she says at last. "I didn't mean to be such a bummer. On your coronation day and everything."

I wave off her apology. "It was inevitable," I say. "All of it." I meet her eyes. "Wasn't it?"

She nods slowly. "I guess it was," she says. "Even though I'm all about free will and stuff, yeah. Neither of us had a choice."

I pat her hands and stand. "In that case," I say, forcing brightness into my voice, "I'd better finish up before they send guards for me."

She grins. "We could just take off." Her hands flap in front of me. "Somewhere, dunno. See what kind of trouble we could get into?"

I laugh and kiss her cheek. "Wouldn't that be something?"

She lets out a gust of air and shrugs before hugging

me again. "See you when you're queen, I guess?" Her hesitation breaks my heart.

"No guilt," I say. "From either of us. This is what it is and I will make the best of it, as you have."

"Not so bad, really, once you're used to it." She heads for the door before turning, hand on the doorknob. "At least we have each other to commiserate."

I let her go without answering, heart heavy. I'm about to let a few tears fall when the door stirs past her retreating form and Femke peeks in.

"Bad time?" I shake my head, smiling for real as I usher her inside. The European leader comes to me, embraces me. "I wanted to see you before it's all official." She sounds sad, too.

Which makes me snap out of my funk. "Why are we all treating this coronation like I'm going to my funeral?"

Femke looks startled, then laughs. "I have no idea," she says. "Except there are those of us, I guess, who know what leadership is really like. And wouldn't wish it on our worst enemy." Her lips twist in a wry smile. "At least I have some amazing people to rule the world with."

We part after a moment, Femke leaving me to dress. "You look beautiful," she says before closing the door.

I catch my mother's scent as she speaks, turning to find her standing at my window. "She's right."

THIRTY

I've always been told I look like my mother and now I see it. Her own blonde hair is darker, but her face shape, the tilt of her eyes and the width of her mouth are all mine. I cross slowly to where she stands, glancing out at the balcony. "You could have used the door."

She smiles, touches my cheek with one hand. "I've grown so used to the sly ways of wolves," she says, "it seems odd to do anything so direct."

"I'm just glad you're all right." My tears spill at last, hands covering my face, the shame of my weakness. She embraces me, whispering soothing words in my ear until I fall silent and wrap my arms around her.

"I am so proud of you, Sharlotta," she says. "I have watched you, as best I could, since your friend Sydlynn freed me from the animal mind that held me silent, all those years ago." She leans away, strokes the tears from my cheeks. "I tried so hard to reach you," her own despair hovers behind her eyes, "and there were times I thought you suspected."

I should have. I feel her now, and know had I only been a little more curious, spent a bit more time investigating... but even her scent had changed, shifted to a wolf, a musk she will, I think, carry with her now forever.

"I raised you to be strong," my mother says, stepping away from me, eyes locked on the tiara I will wear—and have taken from me—when I sit on the throne with a new crown on my head. "To never show fear in the face of danger. And to accept your place as the proudest of daughters of the Moreau family."

I nod. "Thank you for that."

She turns on me with a scowl. "No," she says. "Do not thank me." She runs a shaking hand over her face. "I did you a disservice, my beautiful one. I taught you to be a servant."

"You saved my life so many times," I tell her, hands outstretched to touch her but she pulls away with sharp shake of her head. "Mother, without your teaching, your memory, I would have fallen, broken."

"Never," she says, smiling through new tears. "You were remarkable, even as a tiny girl, Sharlotta. And I weakened you with the old ways of our people." She waves off further protest. "Times are changing, our people with them. There was a point where the greater good of the whole meant more than the needs of the individual." Her eyes are tight with anger, and I wonder who she's thinking of. "But being a wolf, being part of a real pack for so many years, I understand the value of the single soul." She drops her hands to her sides. "And that if we are to progress past our creation, we must release this fierce need we have for outward appearance, let go of our crippling pride and our so-called *can* that has led us to nothing but slavery and dishonor."

What is she saying? I hold my place before her, stunned by my mother's revelations.

"You love that werewolf." She doesn't say revenant, not like everyone else does. "The boy, Sage."

I don't answer. I don't have to. "I have to take the throne," I say.

"No," Danilo says as I turn again to my window and find my handsome, smiling brother standing where my mother had only moments ago. "You don't."

I look back and forth between them, confusion warring with hope and the need to shield my heart from such emotion. "What are you talking about?"

"I would never speak against you," he says, crossing to Mother. He's taller than Father was, almost as tall as Oleksander, but with the soft features of my mother's family, though his hair is as black as our father's. "I will spend my entire life a prince, and happy to do it. You have earned the throne, my amazing sister."

But. He is the elder… how had I forgotten? "Danilo." I choke out his name and he laughs and comes to me, kissing both of my cheeks before cupping my face in his hands.

"If you want your freedom," he says, "as you have so clearly told me you do, I will stake my claim as heir and let you go."

I gape at my brother, the brother I idolized as a girl, saw so little of, never thought to see again.

"There are no promises," Mother says. "Though the pack has accepted us back, they might balk at the idea of your brother taking the throne."

I think back over the last two weeks and suddenly doubt that is true. How did I miss how much the gathering of werewolves deferred to my brother? Worshipped him as he showed them the path to their evolution? This could really work.

"Sharlotta," Danilo says, stepping back to take Mother's hand, the pair of them smiling at me, "I'm willing to try. For you."

Mother jabs him in the ribs, making him flinch away with a grin. "And for you, Danilo."

He nods.

"What does Grandfather think of this?" I half expect

Oleksander to appear at my balcony, but Mother just shrugs.

"We did not think to consult him," she says, eyebrow arching. "That we leave up to you."

The pair exit, through the door this time, but I barely notice. I stare at myself in the mirror, chest heaving, hands clenching the back of the chair so hard I hear the wood crack.

I'm moving before I can ask my body to turn, hurrying out my door and down the hallway. My grandfather's door is at the end of the wide hall, closed but guarded so I know he's in. I pause, nodding to the wereguards before knocking firmly and pushing my way inside without waiting for a response.

Oleksander looks up from his desk, smiling at me as I hurry to his side, rising to embrace me. I hug him quickly, look up into his eyes. He must see my hope because he sags down to sit on the edge of his desk, hands gripping my arms.

"Tell me your next mad plan," he says with a smile. "We've been far too long held captive by our old sins. So, share your escape route, and be free, child."

His fists make hearty sounds against the heavy bag as he strikes it in rhythmic blows. I stand out of the sunlight, not wanting my shadow to disturb the perfection of his silhouette. My eyes travel over his sweating body, naked torso rippling with muscle, a slight tan telling me he spent little time in California after all.

My gaze falls to the crescent scar on his shoulder as the sound of his endless pounding finally ceases. When I look up and meet sea-green eyes full of confusion and pain, I know I've made the right choice.

Was there any doubt?

I casually cross the room, hands in the pockets of my cropped leather coat, looking around with some disdain. "This place could use a thorough cleaning," I say. "Dusty."

"I've been out of town." Sage's deep voice is steady, to his credit.

"So I heard." I stop next to the heavy bag, freeing my hands to give it a soft punch. We're alone in the dojo, though it wouldn't matter to me. The moment I saw him again, he became the only thing in my world I care to think about.

"Charlotte." Sage's voice drops, vibrates as he lowers his hands from fighting stance. "What are you doing here?"

I shrug. "Not allowed, is that it?" I grin. "You do know my best friend practically owns this town." Not really, but Sage knows what I mean.

His shoulders tighten, jaw jumping before he responds. "If you think we can just be friends or something," he says, "I'm sorry. That's not going to happen." He pauses. "Your Majesty."

I'm being cruel, and he doesn't deserve to be treated this way. My hands grab for him as I move forward, pulling him by his wrists when he won't grasp me back.

"Sage," I say. "I have no desire to just be friends. To be 'just' anything."

Clouds pass over his beautiful face. "Then go, please." His tone pleads with me as much as his words. I lean in and try to kiss him, but he pulls away, to the side, though he doesn't fight me. I scent his wolf, his need, and tug harder until my mouth touches his.

He engulfs me in his arms, a moan of desire escaping him, and I can't resist either. We land hard on the mat, my legs wound around him, his body pressing me down into the foam. Sage pulls away from our kiss, my teeth sliding over his lower lip. He pants over me, angry now.

How sexy.

"Sage America," I say. "I would like to petition to join your pack." I release him, lying back. "I am a pureborn werewoman of mateable age and, as far as I know, able to bear more of our kind. Am I acceptable?"

He starts, passion gone a moment as he stares at me with his mouth opening and closing a few times. "I don't have a pack," he finally says.

"Well," I say. "Not yet. The weres you left in California weren't your kind, not really." I stroke my fingers down his naked chest, to the rim of his waistband.

His human mind might be shaken, but his wolf understands my suggestion clearly. "I wasted a trip to California to find that out, though it was nice to check in with Tallah." I snap the elastic at his pelvic bone. "What happened to making sure they don't hurt anyone again?"

He clears his throat, uncomfortable. "Nina challenged me for leadership of the pack."

"Challenged you?" I shift under him, hips against his. "By request?"

Sage's eyes darken. "She'll make a better leader than me."

"Says who?" I shake my head. "They were lucky to have you."

He clears his throat, voice husky when he speaks. "She and Tallah agreed to a partnership, so they are part of the coven now."

I know this already. Tallah told me everything, including Sage's sadness when he arrived, his unwillingness to talk to her. How eager he seemed to escape after only just appearing. I know now standing up for the California pack was a ruse, a way for him to run from me.

Sage doesn't understand yet there is no escape.

My eyebrow arches in playful taunting. "I see. So you shirked your responsibility to flee back here and hide from the world." My fingers slide over his skin again. It's hard not to flip him, pounce on him, devour him while I toy with him further. "I take it Syd was okay with you setting up in her territory?"

His eyes darken past his irritation at my teasing to worry. "I didn't think to ask," he says, voice stuttering. "I have a lot to learn."

I finally can't stand it any longer, flipping him over, my turn to pin him down. "That's why you need me."

He shakes his head as I trace my lips over his cheek, nibbling his ear. He pushes me back, angry all over again. "What are you doing here, really? You're werequeen. You can't just leave and join me."

"Actually," I say, nose pressed to his, "turns out my brother was a much better choice for the throne." Sage freezes, eyes wide. "Even hooked up with his old sweetheart, absolutely adorable, those two." I tweak his nose. "They'll make lovely babies." I close his now-open mouth with a kiss. When I pull away, I've lost my humor, if not my joy, letting my love for him show in my face and through my magic as I wind my power around his. "I was never meant to be a queen," I say. "But I was born to be your mate."

Sage crushes me against him, and I'm weeping on his shoulder as the sun sets through the dojo windows, wrapping us in warmth as our power ties together, forever.

I'm not free. But I never want to be.

Like what you read? Find out more at
pattilarsen.com

Don't despair! There's more from the
Hayle Coven Universe ahead!

Here's a look at the first chapter of
Book One of The Helios Oracles

FORESIGHT

ONE

I walk the streets of Los Angeles with a purpose, though were that reason known, I doubt anyone in my life would understand.

His face is in my mind and has been for as long as I can remember, about as long as hers. The woman I thought was the Dark One. My enemy, my family's enemy, I was told.

I think I've always had a feeling, a private and frightening foreknowledge, that the things I've been told about the future I see aren't exactly the truth.

I pass down Rodeo Drive, ignoring the expensive store fronts, the endless line of flashy sports cars, the chattering women on their smartphones. The sound of stilettos making clicking sounds on the sidewalk as they pass. I have no care for the people of this city, except their existence proves to me I'm real. I'm here. I'm not a figment of my own imagination, nor are the visions I carry inside me some false promise—and curse—of what is to come.

It's so easy to fall into melancholy as I brush past a trio of giggling girls with their perfectly styled hair, tiny dogs perched in dangling bags. Living accessories of the rich and want-to-be-noticed. How simple their lives are, without the complexities of carrying the future of the world in their heads.

I shake out my dark hair as I turn a corner and head for downtown. These stolen moments outside the sanctuary where I live, just walking, are the only real break I have from what I can do. My heart flutters, wondering if he'll show, if I'll see him today or if I'll have to return home before he appears. We've tried to schedule moments, brief but beautiful. It seems no matter our intentions neither of us are able to keep a date.

And so, I risk these trips to the surface just in case he might be here to greet me in the streets of Los Angeles. Though not exactly forbidden to me, my grandmother's hawk eye caution around me makes the sanctuary feel less a safe haven and more a prison the older and stronger I become in my power.

There was a time I felt in awe of the wonders of the world above, and hoped maybe this amazing place would somehow dim the futures I see. But the visions still come, sometimes when I least expect, taking over and drawing me into the fire that feeds them. I don't begrudge my Oracle power, nor do I ignore the importance of what I do, who I am. But there are times I wish this gift had chosen another. A simple life would be so sweet to live.

A life with my darling Piers. I sigh softly to myself as my sandals scuff the sidewalk, his sweet face on my mind.

Then again, were I like those simpering girls, I may never have met him. I bite the inside of my cheek to keep from smiling to myself as I think of the tall, blond sorcerer. Of his angular face and lean body, gray eyes as familiar as my own, the depth of his voice delicious with an English accent. He doesn't know, at least not yet, to what extent I've seen the two of us together. He might be aware of my Oracle power, but I've never confessed to Piers I've been seeing him in my head my entire life.

Piers. I cling to the name, the identity paired with his face. For many years I had no idea who he was, why he was important enough for the visions to show him to me. I had guesses, considering the content of the foresight. My cheeks pink and I cough into my hand, looking left and right with embarrassment as I pass pedestrians completely oblivious to the naughty thoughts running through my head and warming my skin. I've waited a long time to be older, to be the woman I have seen in my visions, the woman he embraces and kisses and whispers of love.

Long enough.

The first time I saw him, in a dark alley not far from where I now walk, I was certain I would blurt out my feelings for him—those ghostly, amorphous emotions clinging to the visions I'd carried with me since puberty struck. Instead, I stared, like a fool. Only the presence of Kayden, the young sorcerer with whom I'd arrived in that place, saved me from making an utter fool of myself.

I still wonder what would have happened if I'd confessed everything to Piers that night, two years ago. To him and his werewolf friend, Charlotte. Instead, I ran from him, from both of them. But my connection to Piers and my worry for his friend woke the visions and sent me a powerful foresight about Charlotte I couldn't resist. I risked everything going to them, sharing what I'd seen about the werewoman and her fate. But even as I did what I could to save her, my heart soared being with Piers, though only for a moment.

I pause at a streetlight, barely aware of the turn of bulb from red to green. My body moves with the crowd as I drift and allow tiny trickles of flame to emerge, searching the city for him as I go. I don't dare let loose my power, not here, even if it might mean tracking him down, being able to spend time with him. Things have changed a great deal since our first meeting, though not as much as I'd like. Not his fault. Mine entirely. It's so hard to break the ingrained fear of outsiders, to share things that I've been told are for Oracles only. It's so tempting to reach out and find him, to let the flames burn and sizzle their way around Los Angeles until I feel his presence. But there are too many magic-gifted people in this city, and I've been taught well enough to keep my presence secret.

"Our family must never be revealed." How many times have I heard those words pass my grandmother's stern lips? "The Oracles of Helios must remain hidden from other magic races if our work is to be unbiased and clean of conscience."

My brow furrows, toe seeking out a small rock to kick into the street as I scowl at nothing. Why, then, the sorcerers, I wonder? Of course, I've never had the nerve to ask, not even when our quiet existence in the vast sanctuary under this city was taken over by a large group of young men, sorcerers all, and their arrogant and watchful leader eight years ago.

I take a break at a small café, sipping hot coffee from a small mug delivered by a smiling, stunningly beautiful barista. This city is full of women and men like her, come to chase a dream of fame and fortune in film and television. As her fingers brush mine, I catch a glimpse through flame of her, older, thinner, face marked and bruised, unconscious in a grungy bathroom with a needle in her arm. I jerk away, though she doesn't seem to notice, and sigh out a soft puff of smoke. Perhaps there is something I could do to help her, if I were permitted. And then again, perhaps not. The lives of normals seem so much more set in stone than those of other races, races with power, as though magic lends itself to flexible destiny.

My fingers drum on the sides of my cup as I people watch, giving up at last on seeing Piers this trip above. I try not to let the disappointment ruin my brief freedom. I have so little time before my grandmother comes looking for me and I don't want her to catch me with him.

That would be a disaster. While he's a sorcerer himself, I'm certain my stern and commanding matriarch would never understand my love for an outsider.

Cup of coffee done, I move on, the complexity of my life turning my mind, as it often does when I'm here, above ground and away from the influence of my family. My first meeting with Piers has led me deeper into doubt than I ever thought possible, and has only increased my anxiety. Not because of him specifically, or the werewoman, Charlotte, whose future I saw with such clarity I couldn't help but assist her. But because of the other face which has haunted me since I was very small.

I shudder despite the heat of the day when her blue eyes open in my mind. There was a time I thought I understood the reason for the visions, with her serious but beautiful face, her dark hair in a messy ponytail, the way everything about her pulsed with power.

My grandmother and her sorcerer mate both pounce on every single instance of vision that deals with her. And I long believed, because of their urgings and interpretation of my vision, this mystery woman was meant to bring about the end of the world.

As a girl, I found it hard to accept, my innocent heart liking her on impulse. But who was I to question Sibyl, the woman who raised me, my own grandmother? For years I allowed no thoughts to the contrary. I glance sideways into the glass of a small shop, catching my reflection, my sad, dark eyes, hunched shoulders. Meeting Piers and Charlotte changed everything.

I slip my hands into the pockets of my cropped jacket, fingers encountering the silver lighter I've carried since I can remember. It was my mother's. The only thing I have left of her, and I cling to it as I turn another corner, head down another street, already lost to the sprawl of Los Angeles. My mind wanders elsewhere as my feet carry me into the deepening afternoon. It's never dark here, the street- and headlights shining over everything, illuminating the city as though it's just another kind of daylight. I slip my thumb over the cover of the smooth lighter and think of home.

I really need to go back. It's almost time for dinner and Sibyl will be looking for me. She's only caught me above twice, making it abundantly clear how disappointed she was to do so. And I don't relish her glare or coldness, or her veiled threats to confine me below. I've never taken such seriously, but I know better than to push her.

And yet, returning too soon means losing any chance I have of seeing Piers today. And if I go home now, Sibyl might find an excuse to sit me in the chapel and push me into foresight. It doesn't matter to her the things I see haven't changed much in several years. I'm just not in the mood to deal with her right now.

Regardless how many times I dissect and review the visions, I can't bring myself to believe the explanations handed to me by my family. Doubt clouds my mind as much as my heart, because something does not seem right.

It was hard to admit to myself, the night I first met Piers and his werewolf friend, Charlotte, that something was very wrong. Despite my deep-seated worries, carried with me all the days of my life, I didn't want to believe my family had been deceiving me. Other Oracles have seen what I have, if not as intensely or with such regularity. But we've all been told the same story for as long as I can remember: the woman with the blue eyes and the serious, lovely face is the enemy and we must guard against her.

Why, then, does her gaze seem so kind? Even when she's destroying the world in my visions, her expression is empathetic, broken with grief. I can't bring myself to trust the word of the family anymore, though I wish things were different. But I wouldn't rewind to that night and never meet Piers. He is my destiny, the other half of my heart.

And I've spent two years stealing brief moments with him.

A fire flickers to my right and I turn to stare into the joyful flames. Fire is my friend, the carrier of the visions, my traveling companion and constant warmth. I drift toward the underpass and the barrel of burning trash, staying out of the sight of those who gather around it. Homeless men and women cooking who knows what over the climbing flames. I see Piers's face in the fire, unbidden, hear his voice in my head, but it's just a memory, not a true vision. If it were, I wouldn't be aware of the rough concrete under my boots or the breeze pushing hair across my cheek.

I touch my lips with trembling fingers, feeling tears well. I've done my best to hide my doubt from the family, but with every day that passes, it grows more difficult and I feel rebellion grow. I'm tired of taking the word of my grandmother at the value she presents, the constant assurance I'm doing the right thing using my power to help her and the others plot to save us all. Because I fear, from what Piers has told me, they have been lying to me my entire life and now I don't know what to do about it.

I turn from the fire, kicking at a small stone, hearing it bounce across the street before I continue on. The flames beg me to return, but I resist. Along with the worry I'm being deceived, the pull of the fire has grown in the past two years. I can still control it, of course, but its call is a song in my heart, begging me to embrace it fully, something I can never do. I know it's a risk. There have been Oracles lost to the flames, devoured completely by the power that is meant to serve us. I am too strong to allow it to happen to me.

At least, I keep telling myself that's the case.

I reach the bottom of the street and slip into the shadows. This is a bad part of town, one I visit frequently, the exhilaration of visiting a dangerous place pushing back my fears about my life. I'm in no real peril. One flick of my lighter and I'm gone, traveling the flame back home, or anywhere else I'd like to go. But being here, where the sound of gunshots is as frequent as the call of sirens, I feel alive. Present.

Not some Oracle who is only good for viewing the future. But here, Zoe Helios, a person like any other, with meaning to her life outside the obvious.

Twenty-one years living for the flame and the visions has left little room for *me*. And the more I explore, probe, examine the things I've seen, the harder it is to resist the fire. But I must know the truth. My heart won't let me get this wrong.

I'm about to turn around when I feel him and everything stops. Ahead, he's there, I know it and the knowledge almost chokes me. I see him emerge from between two buildings, long, gray coat hanging to his feet, lean shoulders back, blond hair over one shoulder, falling in rippling silk to his knees. Those gray eyes greet me with joy, his lean hands already reaching out to me.

He turns, heads my way from the other side of the street. Coming closer. My lips are turning into a smile, my heart beginning to race, even as a mind touches mine.

Zoe. I close off immediately at the sound of Sibyl's cool curiosity. *Where are you?*

Coming, Grandmother. I panic, chest tightening around my sudden nerves. What do I think will happen if she finds out about Piers? I don't dare find out, just in case. She knows nothing of him or my visions of us together. I want it to stay that way.

I raise my hand to him, sorrowful and see him slow, stop. He nods, blows me a kiss. And lets me go.

I'll see you soon, he sends, his dark power embracing me a bare moment. I wish he hadn't. It makes leaving so much harder.

I jerk the lighter from my pocket, flipping open the lid. He doesn't make a sound, standing no more than ten feet away with his hands in the deep pockets of his coat. He watches with calm, adoring eyes and a small smile. One hand rises in farewell even as I strike the flame.

And dive into it, terrified my grandmother might take him away from me, after all.

ABOUT THE AUTHOR

Everything you need to know about me is in this one statement: I've wanted to be a writer since I was a little girl, and now I'm doing it. How cool is that, being able to follow your dream and make it reality? I've tried everything from university to college, graduating the second with a journalism diploma (I sucked at telling real stories), am part of an all-girl improv troupe (if you've never tried it, I highly recommend making things up as you go along as often as possible). I've even been in a Celtic girl band (some of our stuff is on YouTube!) and was an independent film maker. My life has been one creative thing after another—all leading me here, to writing books for a living.

Now with multiple series in happy publication, I live on beautiful and magical Prince Edward Island (I know you've heard of Anne of Green Gables) with my very patient husband and multitude of pets.

I love-love-love hearing from you! You can reach me (and I promise I'll message back) at patti@pattilarsen.com. And if you're eager for your next dose of Patti Larsen books (usually about one release a month) come join my mailing list! All the best up and coming, giveaways, contests and, of course, my observations on the world (aren't you just dying to know what I think about everything?) all in one place: http://smarturl.it/PattiLarsenEmail.

Last—but not least!—I hope you enjoyed what you read! Your happiness is my happiness. And I'd love to hear just what you thought. A review where you found this book would mean the world to me—reviews feed writers more than you will ever know. So, loved it (or not so much), **your honest review would make my day**. Thank you!